"Are you good with that gun?"
Diego asked Raider warily.

Raider had two of the men line up six lighted candles on a bench against one wall. Six candles, the flames rising from them straight and clear. Standing a dozen feet away, Raider let the tension build, then drew the big Remington and tore off six quick shots.

The heavy repart of the forty-four reverberated deafeningly inside the room. A dense cloud of gunsmoke hung in front of Raider as he began reloading his pistol. All of the candles were still upright, but not one was still lighted. Raider had shot out the flames without touching the candles.

"Ay! Que Macho!"

MAXIMILIAN'S GOLD

BERKLEY BOOKS, NEW YORK

MAXIMILIAN'S GOLD

A Berkley Book/published by arrangement with
the author

PRINTING HISTORY
Berkley edition/November 1985

ISBN: 0-425-08280-6

A BERKLEY BOOK ® TM 757,375
Berkley Books are published by The Berkley Publishing Group,
200 Madison Avenue, New York, N.Y. 10016.
The name "BERKLEY" and the stylized "B" with design are trademarks
belonging to Berkley Publishing Corporation.

PRINTED IN THE UNITED STATES OF AMERICA

CHAPTER ONE

It was hot. Miserably muggy hot. Clouds of flies rose from the damp piles of horse droppings in the street. A sour exhalation seeped from the open doorway of a tannery. A huge beer wagon ground slowly past, its iron-shod wheels thundering against the uneven cobblestones. "I hate this fucking place," Raider snarled.

"Tolerance, Raider, tolerance," Doc replied dryly.

The two men were making their way down a crowded Chicago street. They were an incongruous pair: Raider, tall, leather-hard, windburned, dressed in dusty trail clothes, his battered leather jacket hanging just short of the smooth walnut butt of his Remington .44, which rode low on his right hip in an oiled and well-worn holster. His jeans were tucked into the tops of a pair of scuffed calfskin Middleton boots. Doc, on the other hand, was the picture of sartorial elegance, from his brightly polished kidskin half-boots to the crown of his rakishly slanted, curl-brimmed pearl-gray derby. His beautifully cut vicuña suit looked as if it had just been pressed, although he had only a short time before climbed off the same train as Raider, the train they'd been on for the past two days.

Raider swore again as a burly butcher, lugging a haunch of cow over his shoulder, bumped into him on the crowded sidewalk. "Son of a bitch," Raider snarled, turning around and cocking his fist. Doc put a restraining hand on his arm. "It was an accident, Raider."

"Accident, hell! I'll show him an accident. Clumsy bastard got my jacket dirty."

Doc looked at the battered leather. "How can you tell?" he asked bemusedly. By then, the butcher was far out of range and Doc had little difficulty in guiding his partner further along the street.

"Damned place makes me nervous," Raider muttered.

1

"Too many fucking people. Too damn much noise. I couldn't *live* like this."

It was not the most charming scene. The street *was* crowded, it was noisy, the street sweepers had not been by recently, and a noxious miasma rose from the mingled horse shit and urine that had turned the center of the street into a mushy nightmare. And there was the heat, a sticky horror that had soaked into the big stone and brick buildings, radiating out at anyone unlucky enough to be on the street at this early afternoon hour.

"It's progress, Raider," Doc insisted. "The wheels of industry turning."

"Bullshit. Feel like I'm in a zoo. Can't wait to get back out where I belong. Back to paradise."

"Ah, yes . . . paradise," Doc said acidly. "Some miserable little burg in the middle of nowhere, where they'd roll up the sidewalks every evening . . . if they had sidewalks. Where the high point of local culture consists of two drunken cowhands singing trail songs in between puking up cheap rotgut. Paradise? Raider . . . it would be upgrading places like that if you called them *purgatory.*"

He half expected a nasty rejoinder from Raider, but the big man had stopped dead in the middle of the sidewalk, creating a small traffic jam. A well-dressed man snarled something unpleasant and tried to push by. Raider unconcernedly shoved him off the sidewalk into a pile of still-steaming mule shit. Doc knew it was mule shit because he'd watched the mule deposit it there.

The well-dressed man skidded on the slimy cobblestones, nearly going down, saving himself only by grabbing hold of the sleeve of a middle-aged woman, dragging her off the sidewalk and into the street in the process. He might have gone for Raider, but the middle-aged woman began hitting him over the head with her purse, screaming something about rape.

A crowd began to grow, of course, but Raider was oblivious to it all. Doc saw that his partner was staring intently into the dark interior of a saloon. "Oh, no," Doc hissed. "No, Raider, don't do it."

Raider was already pushing open the bat-wing doors. "I got to, Doc," he insisted. "I can't face the old man sober."

Doc followed his partner into the saloon. He had to admit that it was an improvement over the street. Cooler by far. However, they had not gotten more than three feet inside the door before the bartender came rushing around the end of the bar toward them. "Hey, cowboy," he said to Raider. "No guns allowed in here."

"I need a drink," Raider insisted hotly.

"You can drink," the bartender shot back. "But you check your iron at the bar."

Raider hesitated. He hated to part with his hardware, but he did want that drink. "Okay," he said grudgingly as he unbuckled his gunbelt. "But I want it hangin' where I can see it."

The bartender took the gunbelt and, moving around behind the bar, hung it from a peg, next to the big mirror that filled most of the wall behind the long mahogany bar. Raider leaned against the other side of the bar and ordered a whiskey and a beer. Doc sighed and ordered brandy.

Raider poured most of his beer down his throat in one long gulp, then followed it with the whiskey. Doc watched his partner's body shudder from the impact of the rotgut. A satisfied sigh followed. "Set 'em up again, barkeep," Raider said.

While the bartender was drawing another beer, Doc moved over to a table set against the saloon wall and sat down. Raider remained standing at the bar, a pleased smile softening his rawhide features. The smile slipped only a little when a burst of snickering came from a table further back in the gloom.

Both Doc and Raider had been aware that they were not the only ones in the bar. A half-dozen rough-looking men were sitting around a large table, nursing beers. They did not appear to be workingmen. While their faces were hard and brutal, some of them were dressed expensively, if flashily.

"A rum-lookin' couple o' nothin's," one of the seated men said with a sneer, jerking his chin in Doc and Raider's direction.

Raider's smile broadened, his black eyes sparkling, his jet mustache twitching at the ends.

"Raider..." Doc cautioned.

"Shut up, little man," one of the strangers said, slowly getting to his feet. "You'll talk when spoken to."

Doc, who had been trying to warn Raider away from one of his seemingly endless fights, was suddenly very still. "I don't remember addressing you," he said coldly to the man who had stood up. He was a big man, bigger than Raider and much bigger than Doc.

"You don't listen good, do you?" the big man said, walking toward Doc's table.

"I hardly pay attention to every dog that barks," Doc replied evenly. Only the hard narrow glint of his eyes showed his annoyance.

The big man stopped dead, his face flushing with anger. "You callin' me a dog?" he snarled.

"How amazing," Doc murmured. "You *do* understand English. Although you speak it poorly enough. Australia, I assume."

The big man leered. "Sydney, mate," he replied with a high, adenoidal Australian accent.

"Sydney Duck," Doc said casually. "I thought they'd strung up the last of you years ago. Missed one, I see. Too bad."

The Sydney Ducks were a gang of Australian thieves and murderers who had come to the United States during the California gold rush, twenty-five years earlier. Eventually, after a number of atrocities, the San Francisco Vigilance Committee had indeed strung up a number of the gang. The man facing Doc was old enough to be one of the original Ducks, in his late forties or early fifties, hardly an attractive specimen, big-bellied and with a battered face, but he appeared to be powerful underneath the surface flab. And huge, as he moved up to Doc's table and towered over the smaller man. Doc remained seated, even sipping a little of his brandy.

"You got a big mouth, little man," the Duck hissed between his teeth.

Doc looked back up at him and smiled, although it was clear the bigger man was going to hit him. The whole room saw the punch coming, the bunching of the muscles in the Duck's massive shoulders, the shuffling of his feet. The entire beginning of the punch appeared to be in slow motion: the attacker's beefy arm starting its swing down at Doc's unprotected head, Doc raising his glass toward his lips again . . . and then he was suddenly moving, flinging the remainder of the brandy into the big man's face, at the same time slipping sideways out of his chair, moving in a crouch. His attacker's fist swung wildly over his head. As Doc stood up he sank his right fist deep into the Duck's massive belly. "Uuunnnpppphhhh!" the Duck grunted, hunching forward and wheezing for air. Doc moved out into the open, calmly taking off his derby and setting it down on a clean tabletop.

One of the other men sprang to his feet and moved toward Raider.

"You stay out of this," the man snarled. "Don't try helpin' your buddy."

Raider continued lolling unconcernedly with his back against the bar, one boot heel hooked up over the brass rail. "Don't hardly think he's gonna need no help. Not 'gainst that tubba lard," he said amiably.

"Fat chance, cow-lover," the other man guffawed. It did indeed look, at least on the surface, as if Doc were in considerable trouble. His opponent had at least seventy-five pounds on him and was now moving forward crablike, his meaty arms held out toward Doc in a semi-wrestling style.

Doc casually brought his own arms up, bouncing lightly on the balls of his feet. "Either do something or sit down," he said cheerfully. "My friend and I have an appointment, and I really don't care to dance."

"Why . . . you duded up little shit!" the big man bellowed, and lunged at Doc, his right arm swinging. Doc quickly shifted to the side, once again ducking under the punch. When the Duck turned toward him again, Doc's left stabbed out twice, his fist making contact with his attacker's face, two meaty smacks filling the room, red splotches of insulted flesh mottling the big man's face. He snarled and came forward. Once again a series of quick jabs, and now his nose was running blood. He raised his hand to his face, saw the blood when he took it away, and now he lost what little remained of his cool and, with a hoarse cry, rushed in at Doc again.

Once more Doc moved to the side. His right hooked into the big man's ribs. He grunted and bent forward. Doc's right lifted, then planted against his cheekbone. This time the sound was a sharp crack. The big man stumbled backward, and Doc followed, his fists digging into his opponent's body, shaking the fat, bruising the muscle beneath.

"Why . . . the little son of a bitch," the man facing Raider growled, starting in Doc's direction.

But Raider reached out a hand and pushed him back. "Like you said," he murmured, still smiling, but his voice hard, "let' 'em fight it out."

"Get outta my way, shithead," Raider's man said. He had a nearly empty beer mug in his right hand, and he suddenly smashed it against the bar. Bits of broken glass mixed with beer foam flew, and he was coming toward Raider, the jagged beer glass aimed at Raider's face. Raider calmly threw his own beer mug, bouncing it off the other man's face, and while his head was back, Raider kicked the man in the kneecap with the pointed toe of his boot. The man howled, dropping his mug. Raider hit him in the face, driving him back. The man, who was even bigger than Raider, staggered back along the bar—right opposite the point where Raider's pistol was hanging. "I'm gonna kill you, you bastard," he snarled, one long arm reaching across the bar toward the butt of Raider's .44.

Raider immediately leaped forward, steel flashing as he jerked his bowie knife from its sheath along his leg. His opponent had his left hand braced on the bar as his right stretched for Raider's pistol. The knife came down, thudding deep into the wood of the bar, passing through the other man's hand, pinning it to the mahogany. The man howled in agony. He already had the butt of Raider's Remington in his hand. Raider smashed him in the face, knocking him backward again, making his hand jerk against the knife blade. The steel tore through his hand, opening a gash nearly to the wrist. He screamed again and the gun fell behind the bar. Raider ended it by kicking him in the face as he sank toward the floor.

Meanwhile, the tide was turning against Doc. He had continued to hammer his bigger opponent, untouched himself, but by now his back was to the table containing the remaining four thugs. One of them leaped up and pinned Doc's arms to his sides from behind, lifting him half off his feet. The man facing him, his face running blood, immediately lashed out, his fist catching Doc on the side of the head. Doc slumped, sagging downward against the grip of the man behind him, who began to relax a little, grinning as the man in front of Doc moved in closer to hit him again, but Doc was not as out of it as he was pretending to be. He suddenly clubbed his fist backward into the crotch of the man holding him, while at the same time stomping his heel down into the man's instep. The man howled, bending forward as he let Doc go, his own face catching the blow that had been meant for Doc.

It was a general melee now, the only one completely out of it being the man Raider had kicked in the face. Five against Doc at first, because the rest of the thugs had leaped up from their table now and were surging into the fray. Doc circled and weaved, trying to keep them from coming at him all at once, managing to land a blow or two, but having his hands full simply staying out of the way of their wild punches.

Raider reached over the back of the bar and took hold of his gunbelt. The holster was empty, of course, his .44 lying somewhere out of sight on the litter of broken glass behind the bar, but the loops of the belt were filled with long, heavy .44 ammunition, the lead bullets giving weight, the brass cases sharp and shiny. Raider grabbed the holster and began using the entire gunbelt like a flail, charging into the mass of men in front of him. Men howled with pain, backing away. Blood and bullets flew. Doc kicked one of the men in the groin, then planted a hard right into his face. When Raider had the men in front of him adequately stunned, he dropped the gunbelt and waded in with his fists and boots, laying out one man after another.

There was only one man still on his feet, backing groggily away from Raider, when Doc noticed movement from the other side of the bar. It was the bartender, groping on the floor for Raider's pistol. Doc leaped toward the bar, his right hand disappearing inside his suit jacket and reappearing holding a little Smith and Wesson pocket .32. By the time the bartender had Raider's .44 above bar level, the cold muzzle of the .32 was pressing against the side of the bartender's nose. "Think about it for a minute, friend," Doc said in a soft silky voice, the awful snick of the .32's hammer adding a deadly emphasis to his words. The bartender gulped and very carefully set the Remington down on the bar top. Doc scooped it up. The .32 smoothly disappeared back inside his coat. "Time to go, Raider," Doc called out.

The fight was over now, nothing remaining but bodies littering the floor and draped over tables. Raider was scrambling around on his knees, pawing through the filthy sawdust, looking for the cartridges that had spilled from their loops. "Damn things cost a fortune," he muttered.

Eventually he gave up, having recovered about half of them. He buckled on the gunbelt. Doc handed him back the .44 and it went into the holster. The two of them backed toward the door. "Hey . . . wait! You didn't pay for your drinks!" the bartender shouted.

Doc pointed to the toughs, some of whom were staggering to their feet. "It's on them," he said cheerfully, and then he and Raider were out the door and gone.

CHAPTER TWO

"Raider . . . we've *got* to go in."

"Gawd, Doc, I'd rather face down a passel o' Comanches full o' firewater."

There it was, ahead of them, at the top of the stairs, the door with the name on it in a big arc of letters: PINKERTON NATIONAL DETECTIVE AGENCY. Underneath the name was a picture of a single huge eye, and below that the logo "We Never Sleep."

Doc prodded Raider up the stairs. He found the scene amusing, the incongruity of it. He'd *seen* Raider face down a passel of enraged Comanches. He'd seen him stand up to some of the deadliest gunfighters in the country. And now he was afraid of one sick old man.

Doc had to admit he felt a little uneasy himself. That door ahead was not the easiest door to enter.

But he did, with Raider trailing after him. And received the full expected blast the moment he stepped inside. *"Mister* Weatherbee," a querulous voice rasped, in a thick Scots burr. "So guid o' ye ta grace us wi' yer presence at last. Ne're mind ye're nigh onto an 'oor late. An' there's that scapegrace behind ye, Raider."

A moment of shocked silence from the hunched figure sitting at the big desk in the overfurnished room. There was a slight palsy affecting the man's movements, the thick fanned-out beard was more grizzled now, the body appeared smaller than it had been before the stroke that had felled him six years before, but under the craggy brows, the piercing eyes of Allan Pinkerton, America's premier detective, blazed with all their old fire. "Mr. *Weatherbee!"* Pinkerton burst out. "Ye've been brawlin'!"

"Just a small spot of trouble on the way over here, sir. That's why we were late."

Doc took a quick look at himself in a mirror. Damn! His left eye was turning black and blue. By then, Pinkerton was onto Raider. "And you too," the old man said, glaring at Raider's skinned knuckles. The two operatives, shuffling their feet like schoolboys, stood hat in hand in front of their employer, not knowing what to say.

They were saved from further embarrassment when an inner door opened and a tall, heavily built man with a thick mustache and round fleshy face came into the room. William Pinkerton, the old man's son. "Ah, Raider . . . Weatherbee. Where the hell have you been? What . . . the *hell?* Have you two been fighting?"

"Mind yer language, Willie," old Allan Pinkerton snapped. William Pinkerton flushed angrily. He was not the kind of man who took to having others tell him what to say and not to say. But, with the old man, the Founder . . .

"We were jumped by some Sydney Ducks," Doc said quickly.

"Well, I'll be damned. Didn't think there were any of those wharf rats around anymore," William replied, interested.

"Ah, weel . . . that puts another light on the matter," old Allan burst out. "A bad bunch. Why, I remember, back in '55—"

"Yes, Father," William cut in. "Perhaps we'd better get to the business at hand. Now—"

"A rum bunch . . . a rum bunch, but we took care o' them," old Allan insisted. "I hope ye caught 'em in the act."

"Yes, sir . . . in the act," Doc agreed.

"An what's the matter wi' ye, Raider?" the old man barked. "Cat got your tongue?"

"Well, uh . . . no, sir."

"It's certainly got to yer writin' hand. Ye're a month behind on yer daily reports, Raider."

"Well, sir . . ."

"Ye know the rules, Raider. Make yer report every day, even if it's only aboot the weather. It's regular habits that make the regular man, ye know."

Doc committed the tactical error of letting a slight smile

twitch at his lips while he watched the old man demolish his partner. Old Allan suddenly turned on him. "An' *you,* Weatherbee. Ye were way oot o' line wi' yer expenses last month. Ye *know* any expenditure over fifty dollars requires special permission from the head office."

"Well, sir, we *had* to have those horses if we were going to be able to continue the pursuit."

"No irregularities," the old man insisted. "I will not have it, Mr. Weatherbee. Not in *my* agency."

Doc took his chastisement patiently. It was difficult, looking down at this man who had founded the agency twenty-five years before, seeing him in such grievous physical condition. It was, of course, amazing that he had recovered from such a severe stroke at all. Doc thought back to the man he remembered, so vigorous and powerful, the man who had single-handedly disarmed and captured a number of desperadoes. Despite his inner willpower, his strength was obviously waning. Doc glanced at William, who was standing by patiently. He and his brother, Robert, were in effect running the agency now, but the old man wasn't making it easy for them. He'd always been waspish, and tight with a penny, but now that his body was no longer his to command, all he had left was his tongue. Hard to take, sometimes, but he's earned it, Doc thought. After all, he *was* the Founder.

Allan Pinkerton abruptly seemed to tire. "Take them into the inner office, Willie," he told his son, who once again winced. "Tell them what it is we need."

Doc wanted to reach out and pat the old man's shoulder as he and Raider followed big William into the inner office, but he wisely held back. He glanced back at Raider and thought he saw a glimmer of compassion on his partner's normally flint-hard features. Fortunately, old Allan didn't, or there might have been another explosion. He would not tolerate being the object of pity.

To their surprise, there was another man waiting in William's inner office, a tall, meticulously dressed man wearing, of all things, a monocle, which at the moment was suspended from his silk vest by a ribbon. He strode forward, hands behind his back, nose high in the air, looking expectantly at William, then at Doc and Raider. "These are the men you told me about?" he asked in a drawling, affected, upper-class English accent.

"Raider and Weatherbee," Pinkerton said.

The monocle came up to the Englishman's right eye, and for a few seconds he unself-consciously examined the two Pinkerton operatives from head to foot, in much the same manner a prospective buyer would look over livestock, unassailable in the self-certainty of his privileged position.

"Would you like to see my teeth?" Raider asked irritably.

Unfazed, the Englishman continued his inspection, taking in, of course, the two men's rather battered appearance. "These are your *best* men?" he finally asked William somewhat disbelievingly.

"That's what I said," William replied flatly, staring down the Englishman.

Doc treated himself to a smile. Now he understood why William was handling this, and not the old man. Being a Scotsman, old Allan did not have any particular love for the race that had so consistently brutalized his own people. William, being American born, would be more removed from the old man's feelings; but also, being American, he was not about to take any upper-class crap from the rather ridiculous figure standing in front of him.

"This is Lord Crowley," William said by way of introduction. "He's one of the directors of the British Imperial Bank of London. Lord Crowley is interested in using the facilities of the agency."

"Quite right," Crowley said, trying for the moment to fit in a little more with the democratic nature of his surroundings. "Has to do with money, of course."

"Of course," Doc agreed.

"Half a million pounds sterling. In gold."

"Now that *is* money," Doc murmured, impressed. At the current rate of exchange, a half-million English pounds was over two and a half million dollars American. With a meal costing only a quarter, and a workingman lucky to make a couple of dollars a day, yes indeed—a great deal of money.

"The damned Mexicans have it...we think," Lord Crowley said bitterly.

"Uh...maybe we'd better start from the beginning," Pinkerton said. Doc noticed that he seemed to be carefully phrasing his sentences to avoid calling Crowley "Your Lordship." A genuine son of his father, who had once, as a young man, fought for the rights of the workingman in England.

"Of course...of course," Crowley agreed. Chairs were drawn up and all took seats, to Lord Crowley's discomfort, since he was not used to having men like Doc and Raider, or even William Pinkerton seated in the company of their betters—in this case, himself. But, conceding to the customs of the barbarous republic in which he at the moment found himself, he made no complaint. "It all goes back nearly ten years," he said, "to when the French took over Mexico."

"Maximilian," Doc said curtly.

"Yes...Maximilian, Emperor of Mexico," Crowley corrected, insisting on correct titles.

"Not to the Mexicans," Raider cut in.

"Yes, yes...of course. He came to his throne with the aid of French troops, and fell shortly after those troops were withdrawn. Partly at the insistence of your government, as I remember," Crowley added a trifle peevishly.

"The Monroe Doctrine," Doc said quietly.

"Quite!" Crowley snapped tartly. Then, as if attempting to soften his tone, he added, "Never could understand why the Mexican people fought so hard against Maximilian and the French. Maximilian's government did its best to help the common people. Tried to free them from debt peonage to the big landowners. Live as virtual slaves, the people. Damned ingratitude."

"Nobody likes another country invading them," Raider said.

Crowley looked coldly at the proletarian sitting across from him. "Sometimes the obligation of a superior culture to bring civilization to the less advanced is of more importance than mere nationalism," he sniffed.

"Perhaps," Doc said smoothly. "Which is why I could never understand why the English became so upset over the prospect of Napoleon invading and ruling the British Isles, when Napoleon himself proclaimed that he only wanted to bring the liberating benefits of the French Revolution to the downtrodden British masses, who were at the time, if I am correct, living in servile peonage at least as bad as the Mexican peasant's."

Raider shot Doc an admiring glance, as if to say, "Good for you," something he rarely did, since he and Doc were usually on opposite sides of just about any issue that could be named.

Crowley glared at Doc, then hissed to Pinkerton, "Are you *certain* these are your best men?"

"Positive," Pinkerton snapped. "Suppose we get on with the details."

Lord Crowley harrumphed. "Yes, yes . . . well, the British Imperial Bank had a considerable investment in Mexico, which increased during Maximilian's reign. Then the situation started to deteriorate when those damned bandits . . . ah, the Mexican insurgents began to get the upper hand, especially after the French troops were pulled out by Louis Napoleon."

Crowley looked condescendingly toward Doc and Raider. "The Emperor of the French, you know. Napoleon the Third."

"I do believe I've heard the name," Doc replied.

"Well, we at the bank held by our commitments until it became clear that things were going from bad to worse, and finally, in '67, just about the time poor Maximilian was meeting his terrible fate at Querétaro, we decided to recoup what we could, and in the confusion of that terrible time, removed the liquid assets from our branch in Mexico City— the half-milliion pounds sterling I mentioned, all of it in

English sovereigns—loaded it on a pack train headed for the coast and Vera Cruz, where it was to have been put on a boat for London."

"It never made it," Pinkerton cut in.

"Disappeared without a trace," Lord Crowley added. "We quite naturally felt that it had been intercepted by the insurgents, perhaps by some of Juárez's men, or Díaz's. Or, to be fair, perhaps even by one of the Mexican generals fighting on Maximilian's side. They were not always the most trustworthy types."

"A lotta Mexicans called 'em traitors," Raider said bleakly.

"Yes, yes, of course. Well, when Juárez took over, we demanded the return of our money, but he claimed he knew nothing about it, and eventually we believed him. Juárez did not seem the kind of man who coveted money. And since their new government was so obviously bankrupt, we had another reason to believe the gold had not fallen into their hands. The only other possibility was that it had fallen into the hands of bandits, operating independently. God knows, there was enough chaos at the time. Every bandit chief with fifty followers called himself a general. So, we wrote the gold off as a casualty of war and revolution, obviously having disappeared into the anarchy of the times."

Lord Crowley paused, looking down at his fingernails. "But now," he said, graciously adding, "gentlemen, we have information that may help us recover that gold."

"And it's our job to get it back," Pinkerton cut in.

"Where is it?" Doc asked.

"We're not completely sure," Crowley replied. "That's where the Pinkerton National Detective Agency comes in. We'd like you to find it for us."

"You're going to California," Pinkerton said. "Some of the money's been showing up near San Diego."

"It was a special minting," Crowly said. "The gold pieces are quite recognizable. As soon as we heard that some had surfaced, we sent a representative out to California. Working through our banking operations there, along with local banks, we were even able to narrow the source of the money down to one individual—the owner of a ranch in the backcountry."

"Why don't you just have the law take the money back from him?" Raider asked.

"Because we doubt he has very much of it. He shows few signs of being wealthy. He's a Mexican from Sonora, named Mora. Manuel Mora. He used some of our gold to buy a smallish rancho about forty miles from San Diego. It's only a hope, but it is not impossible that this Señor Mora might be able to lead us to the rest of the gold."

"You'll go in under your usual cover," Pinkerton said to Doc. "You too, Raider. Try and find out where that gold is coming from, if Mora has more of it, and if not, where the rest might be."

Crowley looked interested. "What might that cover be?" he asked.

"We prefer to keep that to ourselves," Pinkerton said. Both Doc and Raider were surprised that things had gone this far. Normally, clients were not permitted to learn the identity of the operatives working on their cases, principally for the protection of the operatives.

That was it. Lord Crowley excused himself after one last perusal of Doc and Raider through his monocle, then, nose suitably in the air, he walked regally from the office, leaving the mundane details of the case to William Pinkerton.

By the end of the day, Doc and Raider were on their way to California.

CHAPTER THREE

"Kinda hard to believe all this, ain't it, Doc?"

Doc turned slowly away from the train window and the world flashing by outside. "Why?" he demanded. "It *is* the last half of the nineteenth century, Raider."

Raider looked around at the opulence of the big Silver Palace railroad car: the plush seats, the polished wood, the glitter of the chandeliers. "We've gone further today in this movin' French whorehouse than we could in a week on horseback . . . or in that damned wagon o' yours."

Doc nodded absently, looking back out the window again, watching the flat countryside slip by. Then his face suddenly tightened. "I wonder how Judith is getting along," he said worriedly.

Raider snorted derisively. "Judith, Judith, Judith. That's all I ever hear. You got Judith on the brain, Doc."

Doc looked annoyed. "You'll never understand the finer emotions, Raider." He glanced at his partner, then reached inside his coat, pulled out an Old Virginia cheroot, and proceeded to light it.

"Uh-uh, Doc, not that," Raider protested. Doc looked him straight in the eye and finished lighting the little cigar, puffing a few times, building up a head of smoke, which he slowly blew in Raider's direction. Raider backed off, his nose wrinkling fastidiously. "Gawd, Doc, somebody must be makin' a fortune, huntin' up skunk turds to make them things."

Icy-eyed, Doc blew another puff of smoke in his partner's direction. He knew Raider hated the smell of the little cigars. Sometimes even he had to admit they were a bit strong.

Raider felt a stirring of anger. More than once he'd crammed one of the vile-smelling little weeds halfway down Doc's throat, but he held back now because he knew Doc was only punishing him for talking slightingly of Judith. Doc puffed a few more times, then, seeing that Raider was not going to react, he lost interest in the game and stubbed out the cigar in one of the big brass ashtrays provided by the railroad.

Normally, he and Raider would be riding second class, but this particular train seemed to have a new and gullible conductor. Since the Pinkerton Agency did a great deal of work for the railroads, Pinkerton men were routinely issued blank railroad passes. Doc had filled in his and Raider's for their destination, Sacramento, and had insisted on two seats in the Silver Palace car. The conductor, impressed by their passes and Doc's manner, had agreed. He had even given them a double berth in the big Pullman car farther forward.

"This is the only way to travel," Doc sighed.

Raider shrugged uncomfortably. "Seems too easy to me. Like we're kinda cheatin' in some way."

"It's just the Calvinism that seeped into your bloodline somewhere."

"I ain't got no Calvins in my family," Raider said hotly. "None o' us never could stand that name."

Then, vaguely aware that he probably didn't know what Doc was talking about, as usual, he brought the subject back to where it had started. "I just kinda miss the feel o' the trail. The sun and the wind, and smellin' the grass."

"You mean, the miserable hot sun burning the back of your neck to a crisp, the wind blowing dust and grit in your face, and the stink of your horse and your own body, and the rain running down inside your collar, and freezing your ass off at night, trying to sleep on top of a bunch of rocks and scorpions and rattlesnakes. No, I'll take this marvelously decadent luxury. I love trains."

"You're a real romantic, Doc."

Silence for a while, then Raider said, "You ain't the only one who loves trains. The James boys like 'em too. Hit another one not too long ago."

This sparked Doc's interest. The famous James-Younger gang, which had previously restricted itself to robbing banks, had only a couple of years before discovered how remunerative it was to rob trains. "Makes me sick the way people make heroes out of those murdering thieves," Doc said sourly.

"Well, they did have kind of a hard time after the war."

"So did a lot of people. Wars are like that. And besides, Jesse and Frank both rode with Quantrill, didn't they? They did their share of killing when Quantrill's Raiders wiped out Lawrence, Kansas. Murdered all those civilians. And all those bank clerks and train engineers shot down in cold blood."

"Yeah, you got a point. But they're Southern boys. Lotta bitter people down that way. Anybody who seems to be hurtin' big business and the North is gonna get the hero treatment, no matter what they do."

Doc didn't reply. While both he and Raider had been too young to fight in the Civil War, Raider had been born and raised in Fulton County, Arkansas, and his sympathies were with the South. Doc's Boston background put him on the opposite side, but he was a sensitive enough man to understand a little of the grief that had been visited on the South. He had never sympathized with their stand, but he was not a vindictive man.

Raider cleared his throat uncomfortably. "Doc, you think the agency had anything to do with throwin' that bomb into Mrs. Samuel's place?"

Doc glanced up at Raider, saw the tension in his face. The bomb he was referring to was one somebody had tossed into the house of the James boys' remarried mother. The two outlaws had not been there at the time. The bomb had blown off one of the woman's arms and killed her nine-year-old son.

"I don't know," Doc said. "Some people say it was only a flare, meant to smoke Jesse and Frank out of the house, and that Mrs. Samuels was stupid to throw it into the fireplace. Whatever, it was an unholy mess and can only create more sympathy for Jesse and Frank. A damned stupid move, but then, old Allan Pinkerton and Robert and William hate the James boys to the point of obsession."

"And the other way around. Don't see no end to it . . .

until one side or the other's dead."

"It'll be the Jameses who sack their saddles," Doc said morosely. "A damned mess, the whole thing."

Depressed by the subject, Doc and Raider both fell silent, watching the land go by outside the window. "Lotsa new farms out there," Raider said, watching some nester's shack flash by.

"The country's filling up," Doc agreed, although in reality it was still amazingly empty, with miles between the sparse little homesteads that dotted the prairie. "Hard to believe the United States is a hundred years old. I'm looking forward to the celebrations next year."

Raider's face lightened. "I'm gonna buy me one o' them new Centennial Model forty-five seventy-fives Winchester's bringin' out. Shoots a three-hundred-and-fifty-grain chunk o' lead. That oughta bring down just about anything."

"Including the man who shoots it," Doc muttered. He and Raider had a long-term running argument of big caliber against small caliber.

That topic died too. Raider sank back into the comfortable seat, sipping the whiskey the steward had brought him. Doc tried to relax too, but began to fidget more and more. Suddenly he stood up. "I'm going to go check on Judith," he said, and headed for the end of the car.

"Give her a kiss for me," Raider said, snickering into his glass. Doc ignored his partner and, opening the door, stepped out onto the platform between the Silver Palace car and the one behind it. It was very noisy, the wind rushing by, dirty with soot and cinders from the engine up ahead. Doc caught hold of the guardrail, made slightly giddy by the train's amazing speed . . . nearly fifty miles an hour. Trying not to look down, he ducked into the car behind.

It was a second-class car: big, hard wooden benches, full of people and baggage; babies crying; worn, tired-looking women doing their best to cope; roughly dressed men sitting stoically, arms crossed in front of them, as if they rode the train every day. The working people of the nation, moving west, looking for a better life.

Walking back through the train, Doc passed through two more second-class cars, then through the baggage car, where the guard gave him a curt nod, and then he was in the horse car. He walked down the rocking line of stalls, finally stopping at the fourth one back. His eyes lit up with joy. "Judith!" he said fondly.

The big mule gave Doc a contemptuous look as he tried to plant a kiss on the side of her black velvety muzzle. She did manage to look a little more interested when Doc fumbled a sugar cube out of his pocket and fed it to her. But once Judith had ascertained that Doc had no more sugar cubes, she disdainfully turned away, one of her big brown eyes glaring at Doc. He patted her fondly on the neck, jerking his hand back when she tried to bite him, then wisely let her alone. Judith hated riding on trains almost as much as she hated pulling a wagon.

Speaking of which, Doc went back to the next car, where, by special dispensation, his little Studebaker wagon had been stowed. His name was on its side—a few lines of lettering labeling him a traveling pharmacist specializing in homeopathic medicines, nostrums, patent elixirs, and other various snake oils. This was the cover that William Pinkerton had mentioned and that Lord Crowley had been so interested in. This wagon and its contents would be Doc's entry into the backcountry of San Diego County, which, from all he had heard, was woefully short of the amenities of modern medical science.

By the time Doc got back to the Silver Palace car, Raider was three sheets to the wind. He seldom had the opportunity to drink the quality of whiskey they served on the train. "Looka that," he mumbled, staring out the window.

Following his pointing finger, Doc at first thought he was seeing a huge area of brush that someone had chopped down. Then he realized that the train was passing through an immense graveyard of bones, bleached white by the sun and rain. "Buffalo," he murmured. "What an incredible slaughter."

"Yeah. I heard about things like this," Raider said bitterly.

"Goddamn eastern city dudes shootin' thousands of animals from the train when the herds go by. Just shootin' an' shootin' an' shootin'. Right outta the train windows. Not even usin' the meat or anything. Just letting it all lie there, while the Indians starve."

Doc could do nothing but nod. There was indeed something obscene about that vast expanse of boneyard. "I hear the buffalo are almost gone in this part of the country."

"Yeah. There's still quite a few up in the Dakotas, but I'm guessin' they ain't long for this world. Not now that old Custer's opened up the Black Hills area. That's a dumb move. All that land's holy to the Lakota Sioux, an' they're gonna be downright mad."

"That's what happens when somebody finds gold in a place."

"You just wait. Custer's askin' for trouble, the way he's runnin' wild up there. Never had no use for that show-off."

The whiskey had drawn a pall of gloom over both men by the time they retired to their Pullman berth. Doc sighed with delight as he sank down onto the mattress, thinking of the miles flashing by beneath him, remembering many hard nights on the trail. Amazing, the train. It made it so damned *easy* to cross the country.

The next morning saw them both refreshed. They were entering Utah. Raider whooped excitedly as he saw a group of young Indian bucks whip up their ponies and race along with the train. Then, when the Indians had dropped back on their tired horses, Raider grew gloomy again. "The West has had it, Doc," he said. "This damned train is gonna close it all in. Now that they're gettin' rid of the no-fence laws, there ain't gonna be no open land anymore."

"Can't blame the little farmers for wanting that," Doc said. "They can't have those big herds of cattle and sheep churning up their crops." But as he said this, even Doc, with his love of comfort, felt a twinge of loss as he thought of the old, wild, free, open West becoming just another part of civilization. Maybe at the most another twenty, thirty years.

Night found them entering the Nevada desert. Morning found them still in it, but now the mighty rise of the Sierras was ahead, the eastern wall of California. They both looked out the windows with awe as the train slowly chugged up the steep grades into increasingly rugged and beautiful mountain scenery.

"How the hell'd they do it?" Raider asked in amazement. "How the hell'd they *build* this damned railroad?"

It was a long slow crossing of the mountains, and almost equally slow descending the western slopes. They came out of the foothills in the middle of the night and by morning were deep into the huge San Joaquin Valley, the agricultural marvel of the United States, an enormous expanse of amazingly fertile land that had been waiting for thousands of years for man to bring it water.

"Christ! Never saw so much wheat in my life," Raider murmured.

All around them were thousands of acres of ripening grain. In the distance, outside the fences, the land was dotted with fat cattle. Orchards covered the slopes of far-off rises. Doc had found out from another passenger that they were passing through one of the farms of Henry Miller, a German immigrant who had the largest holdings in the entire state of California. "A greedy, tightfisted bastard," Doc was told. "Takes in millions and won't spend a nickel. He's fair enough to his help as long as they make him money, but he's screwed one hell of a lot of people out of their land. You won't find him winning any popularity contests."

After the vast desert and the high mountains, California's central valley seemed heavily developed. Finally, around the middle of the morning, the train came into Sacramento, a small but bustling city and the capital of California. Doc and Raider stayed only long enough to have Judith and the wagon transferred to a Southern Pacific train headed south. There was no luxury now. This was a work train, bringing men and supplies to the railhead. The tracks only ran south for a short way. The rails were not expected to reach Los Angeles for another year.

They finally detrained just a couple of miles short of rising foothills. Down came the wagon, and down came Judith, complaining mightily. It took both Doc and Raider half an hour to coax the mule in between the wagon shafts, and even then it might not have worked if Doc hadn't bribed her with a generous helping of chewing tobacco.

Raider's current mount had also been stabled on the train, and now he saddled up, swung aboard, and wagon and rider headed south up into the foothills. "Damned fine country," Doc said appreciatively. The hills were not steep, and were lightly covered in a mixture of pine, fir, and scrub oak.

The going was quite slow for the first couple of days. Both Judith and Raider's horse were lazy and out of shape. Judith did all she could to make the going difficult, but by the time they were out of the foothills and coming down into the Salinas River Valley, she too seemed to have recovered an enthusiasm for the road.

It was late October, and very warm. "Just think how it would be up in the Dakotas this time of year," Doc said.

"Snow up to your ass."

They passed the old Spanish mission San Juan Bautista, or Saint John the Baptist, and a few miles later were on the road of the old Spanish settlers and missionaries, El Camino Real. The King's Highway.

Trees were sparser in the Salinas Valley, and the landscape on the whole was very dry, yet here and there large farms already dotted the landscape. Water was being pumped by windmill and steam engine from deep wells. The hills to the east were dun-colored and barren, the ones to the west heavily forested in fir and redwood.

There were a number of small holdings, too, although many of them appeared abandoned, the flimsy shacks that had been homes for hopeful families already sagging, windows gaping, doors creaking mournfully in the breeze.

On the whole, it was a pleasant trip, as they moved slowly southward under the hot sun. The nights were already chilly, Doc sleeping in the wagon, Raider on his bedroll a few yards away. They passed the Soledad Mission, going farther and farther upriver toward the source of the valley. After the first few days, with the stock in better condition, they were making reasonable time, considering the slower pace of the wagon.

Finally the Lucia Mountains loomed ahead. Judith looked with disgust at the steep grade of Cuesta Pass, but she tackled it sturdily enough. At this time of year the weeds and grass were brown and long since gone to seed. The steep hillsides were covered by huge California oaks.

"I like this country," Doc told his partner.

Raider nodded, then pointed toward the steep draws and canyons. "Think we oughta keep our eyes open. Rough country. No tellin' what's hidin' up there."

They made it over the pass in one day and stopped for the night near San Luis Obispo, with its old mission, one of the long chain founded south to north by the pioneer Franciscan monks. The next day found them moving along near the sea, the mighty Pacific, which was curling in pacifically enough at the moment. The air was much cooler, with a tang of salt. Then they were in mountain country again, not as steep as the Lucias, but slow going. It was while they were looking for a place to camp for the night that they saw another wagon stopped ahead.

With a caution born of many violent experiences, Raider drew his Winchester from its saddle scabbard and rested it across the pommel in front of him as he rode toward the stopped wagon, while Doc, following a little more slowly with the wagon, put his sawed-off Greener ten-gauge within easy reach of his right hand.

"Hello the wagon," Raider sang out, aware that whoever was here would have reason to be cautious too.

A woman popped around the far side of the wagon. She stared big-eyed at Raider loping steadily closer. "Jake!" she called loudly.

A tall, bearded man dressed in worn work clothes immediately came around the side of the wagon after her, pushing her back behind him. He had a long, single-shot rifle of Civil War vintage held across the front of his body, his right thumb resting on the big hammer.

Raider stopped his horse. "We're peaceable, brother," he said quietly.

Another man had come around the far side of the stopped wagon. He was holding a Winchester lever-action, one of the older '66 models. He also had an old Colt cap-and-ball .44 revolver stuck into his waistband.

Cautious howdies were exchanged as Doc drew his wagon closer. The lettering on the side seemed to relax the wagon people. "You a doctor?" the woman called out timidly from halfway behind her wagon.

"Traveling apothecary," Doc said. "Why? Somebody need doctoring?"

"Well," she replied, "the kids are kind of a little croupy."

"Nothin' a good meal wouldn't fix," the man with the army rifle said bitterly. "Wagon needs doctorin' a helluva lot more."

Seeing no threat, Raider slid his rifle back into its scabbard, then climbed down from his horse. Doc set the brake on the Studebaker and, leaving Judith contentedly cropping grass, came over to the other wagon.

One of the wheels had broken a spoke. A new one had been whittled and set into place, and now it would be necessary to sweat the iron tire onto the rim. It was late, however, a chore for the morning. The people with the wagon, Jake and his wife, Mary, and Jake's brother, Peter, the man with the old Winchester, and Jake and Mary's three big-eyed, raggedly dressed, snot-nosed kids, two boys and a girl, were on their way toward southern California. It was clear they were not doing well, so while Doc set up their own camp for the night, about fifty yards away from the damaged wagon, Raider took his rifle and rode up into the hills. An hour later he came back down with a big buck deer sprawled across the cantle behind him, much to the disgust and indignation of his horse. Within an hour the animal had been gutted and cut up and big chunks of meat were sizzling on sticks over a fire, while Mary cut up more meat into a big black iron pot to make a stew that would last a day or two. Tomorrow morning, like a good pioneer wife, she would hang cut strips of the venison over a slow fire to make jerky.

The kids ate ravenously, the adults with a little more seemly dignity, but it was clear that all were equally hungry. Doc had a little flour, and that went into the stew near the end for dumplings. The Williams brothers—that was Jake and Peter's family name—produced a stone jug of moonshine, and the men sat around the fire, the world black beyond where its light reached, while Mary Williams put the children to bed in the wagon.

"Headin' down Los Angeles way," Jake said before tipping up the jug and taking a swig of the white lightning. Doc had already decided it would make fine paint thinner. "Had us a place up near Soledad way," Jake added. "Had the papers on it an' ever'thing. Wasn't the greatest spread, but we was eatin'."

He passed the jug toward Raider, then looked into the fire. "Railroad people come along a coupla months ago an' said we was on their land." He said it matter-of-factly, not bitterly at all. Doc suspected the bitterness had been worked out of him long ago. "We showed 'em our papers, but they just tore 'em up an' laughed at us. I knocked one o' the bastards down, but the rest of 'em stomped the hell outta me. Peter was on the other side of our land, which was probably the best thing, 'cause it woulda got to killin' if the sides had been more equal-like. Peter went off to the war, you know. Fought for the South. Peter always was kinda sweet on lost causes. If I'd a gone I'd a fought for the North."

Peter now had the jug. He took a swig, coughed a little, then passed it on to Doc, who merely wet his lips. "I was all for goin' after 'em an' doin' a little shootin'," Peter said. "But Jake said they had the sheriff with 'em. Crooked bunch o' bastards. That damned Big Four that built the railroad— Leland Stanford, Hopkins, Huntington, Charles Crocker— a bunch o' bandits if'n I ever heard o' any, robbin' honest folks o' their land. Between the railroad an' the crooked politicians, a man don't stand no chance around these parts."

"Don't forget the weather, Peter," Jake reminded his brother. Then he added, "Sure . . . famous California, where the fuckin' weather's so good you don't hardly need to wear no clothes, don't hafta work, just pick the fruit off'n the trees an' the grain ripe outta the fields. Hell, just when me an' Mary had got started good, an' Peter was off to the wars, there come that big flood, back in '62. Never *saw* it rain like that. Wiped out the whole damned state. Sure as hell wiped out ever'thin' we'd done. Had to start all over agin, an' then there was one hell of a drought for two years. After that, the smallpox hit. Killed off our two oldest—like to broke Mary's heart. Then the grasshoppers come an' ate up most of our first really good crop. After that, the real vultures—the fuckin' railroad."

There wasn't much more to be said. Times were hard, not only for farmers. The stock market had crashed only two years before. The whole nation was hurting. The roads were full of wagonloads of desperate people like the Williamses. Unbeaten, though, even after having been robbed of their land by the railroad barons, who would not have hesitated to hire men to run them off their land, kill them if necessary, they meant to try again in southern California, where development had not yet arrived.

The next morning Doc and Raider both woke up with a dull pain behind their eyes, a memento of the home squeezin's they'd shared with Jake and Peter. Already Mary Williams was up working at the jerky. The children were helping, stuffing little pieces of meat into their mouths. Groaning, Doc and Raider turned out and joined Jake and Peter in sweating the tire onto the wagon wheel. First the thin iron circle—far too thin—was heated red-hot over a fire, so that it would expand. Then it was carefully sweated onto the wheel, which had been dunked in water. There were great clouds of steam, and as the tire cooled, it shrank tightly around the rim of the wheel, making the otherwise flimsy wooden thing amazingly strong.

The work was done by late afternoon. No point in starting

out so late. Raider potted a couple of rabbits to add to the venison stew, while Doc, wise in the way of herbs, roamed over the hillsides, collecting edible plant life. That night, around the campfire, talk drifted to other troubles in the Golden State.

"They finally hanged Tiburcio Vasquez a few months ago," Jake said. "They got his head pickled in a bottle. He was a real hellion. I know the Mexicans have been robbed even more'n us poor Anglos, but he was a right cruel bastard, killin' an' robbin' the way he did. There's others like him. Hell, half his gang is still loose and said to be headin' down this way. Kinda glad to have you two along."

They set off the next morning, Raider and Doc a little uneasy about the slower pace of the Williamses' big wagon, drawn by its two scrawny, underfed mules, but they had no intention of leaving them on their own in these mountains.

Over the next few days they passed Santa Maria, in its high, lush valley, then headed up into more hills. It was increasingly rugged country.

About noon on the fourth day, Raider, riding a hundred yards ahead, began to grow uneasy. His horse had its ears up and was dancing around a little. Keeping his head fixed straight ahead, Raider let his eyes flicker from side to side. He thought he caught a glimpse of something moving behind some boulders on a steep slope to his left. Trying not to make it obvious, he slowed his horse and let the wagons catch up to him. When he was in quiet talking range he said to Jake Williams, "Think we're gonna have some unwelcome company pretty soon."

"Trouble?"

"Could be. Let's see if we can make it up to those rocks about two hundred yards ahead."

The rocks in question consisted of several huge boulders, some of them nearly as high as the wagon tops. By now everyone in the two wagons was completely alert—the kids, the oldest of whom was nine, the youngest still a baby, big-eyed and silent; Mary, their mother, tight-lipped but not panicking; the two Williams men, grim-eyed, their rifles near at hand; and Doc, bringing up his wagon close on the heels of the bigger one.

They made the rock shelter easily, turning off the main trail, and under Raider's guidance put the right side of each wagon against the biggest boulders, giving effective cover from that direction. Mary and the children were told to lie down on the floor of their wagon and to take everything that would stop a bullet and pile it up around them.

The men armed themselves, Jake with his .58-caliber single-shot army rifle and his brother with his old Winchester. Since Jake had only the one shot, Peter gave him his cap-and-ball Colt. Raider had his Remington .44, which he'd bought only a few months before—it was Remington's most recent effort to compete with Colt's '73 Model Peacemaker—and his lever-action rifle. Doc had his Greener.

They didn't have long to wait. A group of five mounted Mexicans, wearing big sombreros, their bodies crisscrossed with gunbelts, toting rifles, with revolvers stuck into belts or sagging heavily from hand-tooled holsters, suddenly rode out from behind a bend in the trail and approached the wagons.

"Mean-lookin' varmints," Raider drawled to Jake.

"They ain't even Californios," Jake grunted back. "Buncha thievin' scum up from Sonora lookin' for easy pickins."

The five Mexicans stopped about a hundred yards away. Their leader, a big man with a fancy, hand-embroidered but filthy vest, and long charro pants buttoned up the sides, called out, "Why you stop the wagons, señores? You a leetle bit nervous?"

Raider glanced around quickly. "I think there's more of 'em than those five. Probably gonna try an' get the rest of 'em around behind us. Me an' Doc'll face off those five out there. You an' Peter keep a watch in the other direction."

The big Mexican leaned forward impatiently. "I weel not lie to you, señores. We want to rob you. Do not give us any trouble and we will only take your money and your valuables."

"An' your gons," another Mexican chimed in.

"An' maybe your woman, if she is pretty," another snickered.

Raider turned to Doc, Jake, and Peter. "They're gonna try and get us riled up, so we won't pay attention to what's goin' on behind us. We'll pretend it's workin'. Me an' Doc are gonna go out there in front of 'em. Jake, you an' Peter get behind the rocks an' cover our rear."

There were quick nods from Jake and Peter.

"Hey! What's this crap about you and me facing them down?" Doc demanded. "What's this 'we' stuff?"

"Shut up, Doc, and follow me. An' bring that scattergun with you."

Raider, carrying his Winchester casually in his right hand, but with a cartridge in the chamber and the hammer already cocked, stepped out into the open. Doc, swearing sulfurously, something which he seldom did, but which seemed to fit the current situation, followed behind and to Raider's right, the shotgun half hidden behind his right leg, both hammers cocked and ready to go.

The Mexicans laughed and joked among themselves as Doc and Raider moved out about thirty yards from the cover of the rocks, then they slowly nudged their mounts forward.

"Remember, Doc," Raider hissed savagely. "Their horses are probably gonna spook when the shootin' starts. The Mexes will probably shoot high at first."

"Yeah. Head-high," Doc muttered morosely.

The bandits, with their leader in front, drew rein only ten yards away. The leader grinned through his drooping black mustaches, straight at Raider. "I like your guns, señor," he said. "I will take them. And what does the little man with the fancy clothes have behind his leg?"

Raider grinned back up through his equally black but somewhat shorter mustache. "Sure, Pancho. You can have all I got. An' show him what you got, Doc."

Raider let out a sudden whoop, which immediately spooked three of the five Mexican horses, fortunately the ones in front. Cursing, the bandit chief tried to bring his mount under control, then his eyes widened as he saw Raider's rifle coming up. The Mexican reached for his pistol, but Raider shot him neatly between the eyes. The bandit leader was still falling when Raider shot the man next to him, hitting him in the stomach. The Mexican grunted, and managed to pull out his pistol, which forced Raider to shoot him again, costing him time.

Meanwhile, two bandits were spurring their horses around to the side, so they could get a clear shot at Raider. Doc raised his Greener and touched off one barrel. The mass of heavy shot blinded one of the bandit's horses and literally lifted the rider out of the saddle. The second bandit, looking down those awful twin barrels as Doc swung the shotgun onto him, jerked his horse around, giving Doc a side shot. The bandit managed to get off a quick shot just as Doc ignited the second barrel. The bandit's shot missed, but Doc's turned the Mexican's body into hamburger between the waist and the neck. With a last shrill scream of pain and fear, the Mexican flew off the far side of his horse and died on the dusty, bloody ground.

The last shot in that particular fight was when Raider drilled the last of the five bandits through the heart. The man had managed to get off a couple of wild shots at Raider, but his horse was prancing wildly, spoiling his aim. As he fell from the saddle, eyes shocked and disbelieving that this was happening to him and not to someone else, a storm of firing started up behind Doc and Raider from the far side of the rock shelter.

"Come on!" Raider shouted to Doc, heading back toward the wagons.

A dozen bandits were racing toward the rock shelter. Raider heard Jake's big .58 boom, saw a dense cloud of white smoke blossom out the muzzle, saw one of the charging bandits plucked from his saddle as if he'd run into a tree limb. Peter's rifle was banging away with its lighter voice. Two more bandits dropped, but the rest made it to the rocks, and now it was a close-quarters fight.

Raider and Doc raced into the battle, Doc fumbling two fresh shells into the Greener. Men were coming over the top of the rocks. He touched off both barrels and swept the rocks clear. Then more men were pouring around the sides. The action was a confused blur after that. Raider emptied his rifle into the charging throng, missing more than he hit, and then his Remington was in his hand, pumping more lead. He saw Peter go down. A bandit was aiming at Jake. Raider shot him dead. Then another bandit was rushing toward Doc, who was halfway through reloading his shotgun. There wasn't enough time. Doc pulled out his little .32 and shot the approaching bandit in the chest. The bandit grunted but raised his pistol and fired at Doc, missing. Doc shot him in the chest again. And again and again, each shot making the bandit wince, spoiling his aim; but still he came on, until Raider drove him back with one of the heavy bullets from his .44.

Jake was firing his cap-and-ball Colt into the bandits, and then was grappling with one. Another loomed next to him, and then Mary appeared in front of the wagon, an immensely long muzzle-loading shotgun pressed awkwardly to one shoulder. She fired, both barrels, the recoil knocking her back into the wagon; but now the bandits converging on her husband had been reduced to twitching, moaning bundles of shredded flesh.

Most of the bandits were down. One of the last rushed at Raider, leveling his pistol. Raider aimed dead center, but when he squeezed the trigger of his .44, the hammer came down on an empty. Horrified, Raider saw the Mexican grin, saw his finger whitening on the trigger. And the Mexican's hammer came down on an empty too. He screamed in frustration and, pulling out a wicked-looking pig-sticker, leaped at Raider. Raider dodged, jerking out his big bowie. The Mexican slashed at him. Raider simply swept the bowie down against the Mexican's wrist, the long, heavy blade cutting easily through the bone. The Mexican screamed again, holding the stump of his wrist. Raider drove the big blade into the man's belly, upward, toward the heart. The Mexican's eyes bulged with pain and shock, and then he was falling, dying, the desperately clutching fingers of his left hand first gripping, then loosening around Raider's knife hand.

One last double boom from Doc's reloaded shotgun, and when Raider looked around, all the bandits were down, most of them dead. But Peter was still down too. Jake rushed over to his brother and knelt beside him. Raider automatically reloaded his revolver, and a fortunate thing, because one of the wounded bandits rose up onto one elbow and aimed his pistol at Jake's back. Raider shot the man through the head.

Peter was hit badly—through the lung and dangerously near the heart. Everyone could hear the air sucking in and out of the hole in his chest. The blood bubbled pink and frothy. Doc knelt and pressed his handkerchief against the wound, while Raider made the rounds of the area, disarming the few surviving Mexicans. When he got back to Peter, Doc had gone to his wagon for his medical kit.

Peter looked up at Raider and his brother, managing a weak grin. "Went all through that fuckin' war...not a scratch..."

It was clear that Peter was in bad shape. After Doc had done what he could, they laid him in Doc's wagon and the little caravan headed out onto the road again, hoping there would be help ahead. Mile after mile ground on; it seemed as if time were moving with incredible slowness.

Suddenly there was a hoarse cry from inside Doc's wagon, and a moment later Mary's voice, calling out disbelievingly, "He's gone, Jake. Peter's dead!"

A few hours later they came to the Santa Inez Mission. The old buildings, long abandoned, were in poor shape, but there was a little settlement nearby. Peter's body was taken down from the wagon and a priest agreed to bury it. Men were rounded up and were soon riding out in various directions, to alert others living farther out. A posse would soon be heading toward the scene of the battle. Raider doubted that any of the bandits found still alive would escape swinging from a tree limb.

He and Doc left the little family group there at Santa

Inez, grieving its dead, grieving its lost farm and wounded hopes. But Doc and Raider knew that, with the toughness that characterized their breed, they'd make a new start.

"Guess we'll stay round these parts," Jake said. "Nice land here, good people, an' no fuckin' railroad. An' we'll be near Peter."

They stood waving, what was left of the Williams family, as Judith pulled Doc's little Studebaker wagon away along the trail, Raider once again riding alongside. Doc was silent for quite a while. Raider too.

Finally Doc broke the silence. "Now I know why I do the kind of work I do," he said quietly. He looked back at the Williamses, still visible. "For people like them."

And then he was silent again, a little embarrassed. Raider was too. They continued south.

CHAPTER FOUR

The road ground on, down out of the mountains now, making the steep descent through Gaviota Pass, and then they were once again on the Pacific, traveling along a narrow strip of fertile coast pinched between the ocean and steep hills often just a few hundred yards inland. Eventually the little coastal plain broadened out, and they reached the small town of Santa Barbara. It too had one of the old Spanish missions, but this one was in excellent shape. Doc insisted on taking a stroll through the beautiful gardens inside the quadrangle formed by the outer buildings. The weather was still holding beautifully — if anything, growing warmer.

They left Santa Barbara a little reluctantly; trail fatigue was beginning to be a problem. A day later they turned inland at the San Buenaventura Mission. The trail led across a hot, barren plain, with rugged mountains ahead. The way over them was steep, but Judith handled it stoically enough. A day and a half later they came down out of the barren, brown, waterless hills into the barren, brown, waterless San Fernando Valley. They stayed there the night, and were nearly out of water by the time they reached Los Angeles the next day. The *zanjas*, or water ditches, which the Spanish had built so long before, were very low on water, and what they held was muddy and alkaline, but better than thirst.

They didn't bother to stay in Los Angeles. There wasn't much there anyway — a collection of old adobes, a church, a few new buildings. It was a rough town with a bad reputation. Evening found them well south of the town, on the flat Los Angeles plain. The next day, as they headed farther south, toward Santa Ana, they began to encounter small orange groves wherever there was enough water. Doc bought several crates of the juicy golden fruit from a local farmer and stacked them in the wagon. He and Raider ate the oranges from time to time during the next few days, partly for the sweet taste, partly because the juice helped slake

37

their thirst and strip the dust from their throats. It was the end of summer, the end of autumn, both seasons being more or less indistinguishable in these parts, and it was dry, dry, dry, with dust floating up from the trail. The rains were not due for another two or three weeks.

Santa Ana went by. They followed a long fertile valley, which finally came out near the sea and the mission of San Juan Capistrano. "Saint John the Beheaded," Doc mused, translating the name.

"Those Spaniards sure do go in for that kind of talk," Raider muttered.

The next thirty miles were once again along the shores of the Pacific. It was very dry country, with hills marching back from the coast, covered mostly in brush, with willow and live oak along dry streambeds. Most of the terrain inland from the sea at this point belonged to the huge Santa Margarita Rancho, thousands of acres of it. The land became increasingly cultivated, and at last they reached the small beach town of Oceanside. Here they turned inland after Raider had taken time out to stare at the immensely wide, white sandy beach.

A few miles farther inland and they were at the San Luis Rey Mission. "Named it after Saint Louis, the King of France," Doc told Raider. It was impressive, although partially in ruins. The massive bulk of the main building sat blocklike on the flat dusty ground, appearing very much like a ruined palace in Syria or some other part of the Middle East.

Intrigued, Doc insisted they look around a little. It was while they were nosing about inside the partly tumbled-down walls of an old garden that they realized they were not alone. The old cactuses and some of the mimosas and pepper trees, species that could survive well without either much water or human care, had made of the ruined garden a semi-jungle, and suddenly Raider heard the crunch of feet on gravel. As he spun around a Franciscan monk accompanied by a couple of mestizos came walking out into the open.

"Hello, my friends," the Franciscan said.

Doc and Raider greeted the man. To their surprise he did not appear to be Spanish. He was rather portly, with a broad, reddish, smiling face and sparkling blue eyes set rather deeply into their sockets.

The Franciscan waved his arm at the remains of the mission. "Impressive, isn't it?"

Doc and Raider allowed as how it was. They were interested in this man and what he might be able to tell them. They were now not very far from the rancho owned by Manuel Mora, the man who had been spending Maximilian's gold. A little reconnaissance was in order. Their only local contact was a regular Pinkerton informant who lived in the town of San Diego, forty miles farther south. He was a bank clerk whose code name—the agency liked giving its informants code names; old Allan claimed it made them feel more important—was Sassafras. The agency had legions of informants, from tradesmen to lawmen, who regularly reported incredibly varied tidbits of information to the Chicago headquarters, where it was recorded in vast, carefully cross-referenced files. It was from Sassafras that the first word had come concerning the English bank's gold sovereigns surfacing in San Diego County. But with him so far away, this priest might be the best source for gaining local information.

"I didn't know your order still ran this place," Doc said to the Franciscan.

The monk smiled. "We haven't for a long time. I love it here, though. I've loved it for a long time and spend as much time as I can here. I've managed to build up a little parish." His blue eyes looked around at the imposing masonry. "I'd so love to rebuild it."

"You're American, aren't you?"

"Yes. There are not enough of the Spanish monks left. I speak Spanish, though. I wouldn't be a very good pastor if I didn't." He smiled at the two men with him. "Right, Antonio?" he asked one of them.

The man, apparently at least three-quarters Indian, smiled

back shyly. *"Sí, Padre,"* he said in a soft voice.

The two men with the priest were dressed in a mixture of Mexican and Anglo clothing, wearing shapeless American hats, Mexican vests, and baggy work trousers. They wore huaraches, open Mexican sandals, on their cracked and dusty feet. Antonio, the one the priest had spoken to, was fairly young. The other man looked quite old, his reddish-brown face wrinkled like a relief map, but with black, still-snapping eyes glittering curiously at the newcomers.

"These are two of my assistants," the priest said. "They help me with the Mass, or with anything else necessary. You know Antonio's name already. This is Baltasar," he added, pointing to the old man, who bowed, straight-faced. "And I am Father William. Would you like me to show you around?"

After introducing themselves, Doc and Raider accepted the invitation. Father William turned to his two assistants and asked them to wait for him in the garden. They nodded woodenly, but when Doc and the priest had turned away, Raider noticed the two mestizos grinning at one another conspiratorially. Then they vanished behind a huge clump of cactus plants that had broad, swordlike leaves.

Raider hurried to catch up with Doc and Father William. The Franciscan led them out onto the broad dirt expanse in front of the mission. The massive central structure lay before them, with colonnaded archways leading off to the left.

"Imagine all this as it was only forty years ago," Father William said. "Everything whitewashed and gleaming in the sun, people bustling about everywhere, gardens full of good growing things, blacksmith and leather shops busy, riders coming and going." He turned around, pointing to some low ruined buildings behind him. "Over there—the quarters of the soldiers and their families. And out there"—and now he pointed to the broad valley, stretching off to the east—"the herds and cultivated lands. Tens of thousands of cattle, sheep, and horses. Fields of wheat. Grape vineyards. How it must have looked! I've only seen pictures."

He sighed regretfully. "This was called the King of the

Missions, you know. It was the only one laid out in the shape of a cross, and with an octagonal dome over the church."

He pushed open a rotting door in the front of the main building. Inside, the church was damp and cold, but there was enough light to make out faded paintings on the pilasters and on the wooden beam ceiling. "The Indian neophytes painted those," Father William said. "Isn't it lovely in all its primitive innocence?"

Doc and the priest talked learnedly for a while about the style of painting used by the simple Indians to try and picture a Christian mythology they could only vaguely comprehend. Raider's comment was more direct. "How come this place is so damned run down now?" he asked.

Father William sighed. "Over forty years ago, after Mexico had won its independence from Spain and was in control of Alta California, it was decided that the missions would be secularized. There was a lot of liberal feeling at the time, you know, and the ruling group in Mexico felt that it was time for the Indians to be granted the same legal status as anyone else living under the Mexican flag—at least up here, out of the way, in far-off California, where it wouldn't rock too many boats. The Indians are *still* helpless slaves in Mexico itself. There were other reasons here too. Political and business ones. Simple greed. Until the secularization, the missions held most of the really productive land. The lay people simply wanted it, so the missions were secularized. The plan was that the Indians who had been working the land for so long under the guidance of our order would receive half the mission land, while the rest would go to Spanish settlers already here. It did not, of course, work out that way. The Indians, unsophisticated politically, soon found themselves dispossessed and penniless, and ended up supplying a pool of cheap labor for the big ranchers who took over the missions."

"I'll bet there was some trouble over that," Doc said.

"Oh yes. Some of the more bitter Indians joined with the wild Indians of the interior and began to raid the white settlements. It was not so severe farther north, but here, in

San Diego, there were so few settlers—never more than a few hundred—that they could not easily defend themselves. At times they had to abandon their ranches and hide in the San Diego Pueblo. There was now no real military help, either. Before, the soldiers had been supported by the missions, and now there were so few, and for the most part riffraff. Poor San Diego. It was the stepchild of California. Not so many wealthy *hacendados* here. That's what the Mexicans call rich landowners, you know."

"I know."

They walked out of the side door of the church into a small cemetery shaded by big trees. It was surprisingly well kept, neater, in fact, than the rest of the grounds. Doc was walking up front with Father William, Raider following behind, trying to read the faded lettering chiseled into or painted on the gravestones.

"The settlers were not very good to the Indians, you know," Father William said. "They thought of them, and those of obviously mixed blood, mestizos like Antonio and Baltasar, as lesser people. They called themselves, *gente de razón,* literally, 'people of reason.'"

"An' now the Anglos think of *them* as greasers," Raider drawled.

"Yes," Father William said sadly. "Intolerance is so infectious."

"How have the original Spanish-descended settlers made out in this part of California?" Doc asked.

The priest shrugged. "Perhaps as well, or badly, as anywhere else in the state. They quickly lost political power, because they were so soon outnumbered by the Americans coming in. They did not understand that much about voting, and how to manipulate the political process, short of revolution. The more important among them were concerned with honor and appearances. Most of them kept their land, as the U.S. government had promised they would be able to, and some of them even got rich, during the fifties, when they were able to sell their cattle for high prices to the gold miners in the north. But that quick wealth also sowed the seeds of their downfall, because they didn't understand that the good days would not last forever. They far overspent their incomes, mortgaging everything they had so they could put on the kind of display of wealth they love so much. They gambled huge sums, they wore fortunes on their backs and loaded their horses with silver, they bought the most expensive things they could find, and then, when the price of cattle dropped, and the floods and the droughts and the grasshoppers came, they were ruined.

"Even old Able Stearns, an American who married one of Juan Bandini's daughters way back before California became American, went broke. There are lots of people still going broke now. The land rush from back east might save a few. Not their land, but their money. You know, the newspapers on the East Coast run advertising touting California as the land of opportunity. 'Come out and settle down on your quarter-acre of paradise.' There are so very many people flooding in now, little people who can't afford to make mistakes. But they do."

Both Doc and Raider nodded, thinking of the Williamses. The priest led them around the rear of the grounds now, and they suddenly found themselves back in the garden where they had met the priest. Father William looked around for his two assistants. They were nowhere in sight. Then there was the sound of low laughter and clinking of glass. Father William's eyes narrowed in annoyance. "Antonio . . . Baltasar! Come out here!"

Dead silence from the cactus jungle, then the shuffling of feet and the two mestizos slowly came around the edge of a clump of cactus, walking hesitantly and looking guilty. At least Antonio looked hang-dog; old Baltasar was holding his head up proudly. As the two men came nearer, the priest and Doc and Raider could smell the alcohol on their breath.

"The local curse," Father William said sadly. "If we could only exorcise *that* kind of spirits."

Doc laughed, Raider frowning for a moment before he got it too. Father William smiled indulgently at the two delinquents. "Baltasar can remember the old days," he said in Spanish. "Do you understand Spanish?" he asked Doc and Raider.

They both nodded. At least a smattering of the language was a necessity in large parts of the Southwest.

"Would you tell us?" Doc asked the old man.

Baltasar's head came up even further. For a moment he looked like a stringy old eagle, his black eyes snapping, the hooked beak of his nose arching outward. "I remember," he said.

Seeing that all eyes were on him now, he sat cross-legged on the dusty ground, wobbling a little on the way down, but managing it with sufficient dignity, despite his inebriated state. "I do not remember the time when we were free," he said. "The time before the Spanish came. My father told me about it, and my grandfather told me even more. I myself was born on the grounds of this mission. My father herded the sheep and my mother ground corn for tortillas day and night in the mission kitchen. When I was very small I was put to work in the gardens. We were not free," he said tersely, casting a quick look in the direction of the priest. "We could not leave the mission without the permission of the fathers. If we did, they sent the soldiers after us. Sometimes they killed us when they found us. Or they beat us when they brought us back. They beat me whenever I made a mistake, and they told all of us to be the servants of their gods—the man on the tree and the virgin goddess with the baby. My father helped paint some of the pictures in the church. I lived my life here from the time I was born, and then all of a sudden the priests were gone and we were told we had to leave. The *gente de razón* killed some of those who refused; they wanted the land we had made rich, and then we had to work for them as we had worked for the fathers with the brown robes, because we had long ago forgotten how to live like our ancestors. We have been slaves here in our own land for the space of many lives."

Father William coughed apologetically. "I'm afraid some of my predecessors were a little overzealous in converting the heathen," he said. "But most of the mission people are now more or less integrated into the general Californio population. The racism of the Anglos has overcome the racism of the *gente de razón*."

Old Baltasar was left there, sitting on the ground. The priest once again led Doc and Raider out of the garden. Raider saw Antonio bringing a bottle to the old mestizo, who took it unhesitatingly, tipping his head back as he drank, his mind no doubt full of the old days. The priest asked Doc and Raider where they were heading, and Doc told him east. Inland.

"There isn't much back there," Father William said. "However, you will eventually reach the Pala Mission, a much smaller place than this, one of the old Indian *rancherías*, but it is still in service. Father Gregorio is there, a good man, and he will help you if you need help. It's still pretty much the old life back there—vaqueros, ranchos, the old ways. You may not be all that welcome."

"We'll take our chances," Doc said. "Any big ranchers there?"

"A few. Lots of land to be had. There are still absentee landowners down in Mexico. They've been selling cheap for the past twenty years. I've heard that one man, I think his name is Mora, came up over the border a couple of years ago and bought a fair-sized parcel. Paid for it in gold, I'm told. There's precious little of that around these parts, I can tell you. How I'd like to have some of it to rebuild this church!"

Now quite certain that they were on the right track, the two Pinkertons bade goodbye to Father William and his by now well-pickled assistants, and set out on the road east, into California's past.

CHAPTER FIVE

Once they were well out of sight of the San Luis Rey Mission, Doc and Raider decided to split up. It would look a little strange if the two of them moved in on Mora together. If he was the man they wanted, he'd be living with constant suspicion.

"You go on ahead. I'll camp out for a couple of days," Raider said.

Last-minute plans were made. Raider looked at Doc and shook his head. "Still ain't got nothin' on you bigger'n that thirty-two caliber peashooter," he said. "That thing's gonna be the death of you."

"Wild Bill Hickok uses one," Doc snapped.

"Sure . . . as a backup, a hideout gun. Hell, Doc, when you shoot somebody with that thing you just make 'em mad. Get yourself a real piece of iron. This is rough country."

Of course, they were both remembering the fight against the *banditos* farther north, and the negligible effect Doc's bullets had had on the man trying to kill him. Only the heavy hitting power of Raider's big .44 had saved Doc's skin. But Doc hated to have to rely on heavy hardware. He had once told Raider, "If you can't talk your way out of a situation, you're already in trouble."

Raider had shook his head sadly. "There's a lotta gents out this way don't know no language except Colonel Colt's."

They parted, Doc continuing east, Raider riding up into some low hills to seek out a campsite. Doc's road began to climb a little, into rugged and apparently empty country. The ground cover was mostly brush. There were a few dry watercourses to show where water ran when it rained hard enough, but on the whole, it was an arid land.

He camped out for the night, missing Raider's company. Around mid-morning of the next day he pulled his wagon into the dusty front yard of the Pala Mission. It was a little place, with none of the majesty of San Luis Rey. He had barely hitched his mule when the front door of the mission opened and a wizened little Franciscan came out and greeted him in halting English. Doc immediately replied in Spanish, which brought a look of relief to the priest's face. The Franciscan introduced himself as Father Gregorio. He was obviously very curious about Doc. "It is not often that people from the coast get this far inland, señor," he said.

"I have an insatiable curiosity that drives me to search out new places," Doc confessed. "Which is why I am in the business I am." He did not, of course, say what his *real* business was.

When Don Gregorio discovered that Father William of San Luis Rey had recommended Doc, the little priest's manner warmed even more. He was clearly eager to have someone to talk to, especially a man of obvious education such as Doc.

An Indian servant brought wine, cold meat, and tortillas, and the two men sat down on the veranda of the priest's quarters to talk. Under the influence of the wine, which the priest imbibed quite heartily, Doc following his example willingly enough, the mood grew garrulous.

"It has been a very long time since a man of medicine came this way," Don Gregorio said.

Doc gave a few polite disclaimers as to his actual medical ability, but the priest was impressed nevertheless. He told Doc of the difficulties that existed in this isolated mission, which bordered on an Indian reservation, a large chunk of arid, mostly waste land onto which the Indians had been herded by the government in the apparent hope they would die off. Doc could sense the priest's desire for medicines for his charges, but he also sensed that there was no money available to pay for them. Doc graciously offered to donate a considerable supply. Don Gregorio was overjoyed, and called for another bottle of wine, which did nothing to hinder the air of celebration.

It was easy for Doc to get a complete rundown on everyone living in the area. He merely told the priest he would be calling on outlying ranches. Within an hour he had heard

a great deal about Manuel Mora, the man he and Raider
had been sent to investigate. Mora owned one of the better
ranches in the area, not because it was unusually big, but
because it was so well run.

"A good man, Mora," Don Gregorio said. "And a lovely
and virtuous lady, his sister, the Señorita Carmen."

"He has a sister?" Doc asked idly, but the priest sensed
the interest in his voice, and his eyes sparkled.

"A veritable jewel, buried in this wilderness, as is Don
Manuel, both of them people of breeding and education.
True *gente de razón.*"

Doc passed the night at the mission, drinking wine late
into the evening with Don Gregorio, who avidly milked Doc
of every tidbit of news about the outside world that Doc
could think of. Doc set off the next morning, more than a
little hung over. Don Gregorio had provided him with a
little hand-drawn map that showed the various settlements
and ranchos in the area, and Doc began following it from
point to point, restraining himself from heading straight for
Mora's ranch. Most of the places he stopped were very poor,
as Don Gregorio had indicated they would be. For the next
three days Doc put his Pinkerton case from his mind and
concentrated on helping those he met, dispensing herbs and
salves and tonics to a succession of unfortunates, usually
at a minimum cost, charging just enough to protect the pride
of the recipients, usually part of a chicken, or a few tortillas,
and on rare occasions a handful of carefully hoarded pen-
nies.

On the fourth day he arrived, by logical progression, at
the rancho of Manuel Mora. Long before he got to the ranch
hacienda itself he began to see signs of affluence—sizable
groups of cattle, most of them longhorns, but a few of the
new shorthorn breed, too, carefully corraled to keep the
expensive cows from the longhorn bulls.

There were no fences around the ranch; it was all still
open range. Doc saw a few vaqueros in the distance who
looked at him curiously as he went by, but they did not
interrupt their herding duties to investigate him. They were

a colorful lot, all of them apparently of Californio or Mexican descent, wearing low-crowned, flat-brimmed sombreros, fancy embroidered vests, and long trousers with buttons down the outside of each leg, the buttons below the knee left undone so that the bottoms of these pantalones flared out stylishly. Some of the vaqueros wore American-style boots, but some were wearing the old-style soft shoes, turned up at the toes, with leggins above.

When Doc got nearer to the hacienda, which he could see on a low rise ahead under some oaks, a small band of riders came galloping up to him, riding wildly, as he saw it. For a moment he wondered if he was being attacked, and his hand strayed toward the butt of his Greener. But the mad rush of the riders was merely a sign of their general exuberance. They pulled up rein a short distance away, their horses' hind legs sliding up under them, dust flying, the riders yipping happily.

They were obviously a reception committee and an escort. They formed up around the wagon as Doc continued toward the hacienda. He did not see many guns among them; most of the vaqueros seemed content with the knives they wore at their belts or in their boot tops. One or two had pistols stuck into the wide, colorful sashes they wore at their waists. One of the pistols was an old single-shot model at least fifty years old. A few of the riders had short heavy swords tied to the sides of their saddles, resting under their left legs.

When Doc was quite close to the hacienda, he saw a well-dressed man of about thirty-five come out onto the veranda. He stared in Doc's direction for a few seconds, then stepped off the veranda and mounted one of several horses, all of them saddled and bridled, which were tied to a hitching bar in front of the house.

Doc had heard that these rancheros never walked if they could ride, even if the distance was slight. That seemed to be the case now. The horseman had cantered only about fifty yards by the time he reached Doc's wagon. Doc noticed that the men on either side of him drew back respectfully as the newcomer approached.

Doc pulled back on the reins and stopped Judith. She complied quite willingly, though made a little nervous by all the prancing, snorting horses around her. Judith hated horses. Doc stood up on the front of his wagon seat and introduced himself.

The other man gave a little bow from the saddle. "Manuel Mora, at your service," he said politely, but Doc noticed that the man was scrutinizing him intently. "We heard that a medical man with a wagon was coming this way," Mora said.

"Not a medical man . . . just an apothecary," Doc disclaimed politely.

"From what I have heard, you are far too modest, señor. Either way, we will be only too happy to avail ourselves of some of the things you have. Perhaps if you would come up to the hacienda . . ."

Doc urged Judith into motion again, and as his little wagon approached the house, he made a quick but careful evaluation of Manuel Mora as he rode along beside the wagon. He was an impressive-looking man, not from any particular size or unusual handsomeness, although he was well enough formed, but because of the gracefulness with which he moved, spoke, and appeared to think. He was obviously, as Don Gregorio had said, a man of culture and breeding.

They reached the house. A servant appeared to take charge of Judith, and to Doc's surprise his usually cantankerous mule took it all quite calmly in stride. The vaqueros were sent away and rode thundering out of the ranch-house yard, yipping and cavorting, playing little tricks on one another, and in general exhibiting such a degree of effortless horsemanship that Doc was impressed.

"My God, how they can *ride!*" he murmured.

"But of course, señor," Mora replied. "They are Californios. Some of them were on the back of a horse before they could walk. Now, if you would honor me by entering my humble house . . ."

The house was humble only in that it was simply constructed, the walls being of handmade adobe bricks, the roof of dark red tiles. It was a large place, rambling haphazardly here and there, with many additions obviously built on at various dates, more for utility than by overall plan. The house was cool inside, and the rooms well stocked with furniture, some of it quite good. Mora spoke a word to a servant, and while the man went to fetch bread and wine, Mora ushered Doc into a large room with a huge fireplace at one end.

The men had barely seated themselves when they heard the sharp click of heels on the tile floor and a woman entered the room. "Ah," Mora said, getting to his feet. "My sister, Carmen . . . Dr. Weatherbee."

Doc had also risen to his feet and now stood, stunned. He was certain that Carmen Mora was the most beautiful woman he had ever met. She had enormous dark eyes set wide in a fine-boned face. Her thick dark hair was drawn back and tied behind her head, making her eyes all the more noticeable. Intelligence shone from those eyes. At first glance she looked quite slender, but a second glance took in the firm, high breasts filling out the front of her somewhat low-cut dress. She moved with a sinuous grace, hinting at strong legs and well-curved hips.

"Dr. Weatherbee," she said in a well-modulated, somewhat throaty voice.

What the hell is a woman like this doing way out here in the middle of nowhere? Doc asked himself. She would not be out of place in am emperor's court.

Doc managed to bring his tongue back under control and made some polite rejoinder to Carmen Mora, even if he could not later remember what it was he had said. Suddenly this case was taking on a whole new personality. He liked these people, the Moras, his quarry. At the moment his main interest was simply to get to know them as people, and not as suspects in a case consisting of five hundred thousand pounds sterling in missing British gold.

Nor was his interest unreturned, particularly by Carmen.

After the refreshments were brought and they were seated, sipping wine from good crystal goblets, Carmen's huge eyes shone with curiosity and excitement, and once again Doc was called upon to provide news of the outside world. Carmen listened with well-bred avidity. Mora was listening too, but with more restraint. It seemed to Doc as if he were not all that happy to hear that the outside world still existed. As if there were some barrier between him and it. Understandable, if he were the man they were indeed after.

But Doc did not want to think about that at the moment. He wanted only to lose himself in Carmen's eyes, to watch her as she bent forward eagerly, the low-cut dress falling away from her body, giving him a breathtaking glimpse of the swelling curves of breasts surprisingly large for such a slender woman.

Doc was asked to stay the night, an invitation he eagerly accepted. Then they talked a little about Mora's ranch. Rancho La Libertad, it was called. "We are from Mexico, Señor Weatherbee," Mora said quietly. "I call this place 'La Libertad' in honor of my country's independence from Spain. And perhaps in honor of that final liberty when it will someday be free of the thieves and tyrants who now enslave it."

Under Doc's judicious questioning, Mora said that he was from Sonora.

"But only recently," Carmen cut in. "Before, we were from Mexico City. The capital."

There was something approaching reverence about the way she pronounced "the capital." Doc sensed in this lovely young woman, who was certainly no more than in her early or middle twenties, a yearning to return to civilization. Only her brother's obvious displeasure kept her from elaborating on the theme.

Mora pleaded pressing ranch duties. Carmen excused herself, and a servant was allocated to Doc. Within a half hour he was luxuriating in a hot bath, in a large room that was to be his while he was at Rancho La Libertad. He dressed himself in clean clothes for dinner, which was as elaborate an affair as the isolation of the ranch permitted. The food was simple, built around beef, but the wines were good. Doc was seated across from Carmen. She urged more information out of him. How starved she seemed for the world.

When Doc went to bed that night, he was intensely aware that Carmen was doing the same farther down the hallway outside his door. His mind played with images of Carmen taking off that full-skirted dress, baring what could only be beauty beneath it. He remembered those eyes, and the way she had looked at him. He was a long time in getting to sleep.

CHAPTER SIX

Doc spent two more days at the Mora rancho, part of it business, part of it pleasure, and during that time it became quite clear that Carmen Mora was after him body and soul, although it looked like she'd settle for the body at the moment. He knew what she was after. She was bored. She wanted someone to rescue her from her isolation, and Doc, with his education, his culture, and his good looks, was the best candidate she'd seen in a long time.

Carmen was not crude about it. She was, after all, a young lady of breeding. But she was also a young lady of strong will. Normally, all of this would have been a godsend to Doc. After all, he *was* investigating the Moras, and there are few better places to uncover long-held secrets than in bed. Besides, the girl was unutterably lovely.

However, Doc resisted the temptation. His reasons for doing so were complex, as puzzling at times to him as they were to the girl. For one thing, he did not think of her as an easy conquest. There was something marvelously fine about her, as well as something a little unsettling, a latent selfishness that warned him he might get his fingers burnt. And then there was her brother, whom Doc was beginning to like very much. Doc was a professional; he was quite capable of arresting the man, friend or not, if he were to discover he was indeed a thief. But to betray both him and his sister by sleeping with the girl and seducing family secrets from her . . . no, that was just too low.

So he avoided Señorita Mora, or at least insisted on misunderstanding the passionate looks she so often sent his way. He could see that Carmen was getting a little annoyed. She was obviously not accustomed to being rejected once she had made her availability known. Doc was not certain just how far her availability went, anyhow, so, when he finally drove his wagon out of the ranch yard on the third day after his arrival, he left a pouting Carmen standing on the veranda, watching him go. Pouting with class, however.

Doc spent the next couple of days visiting other places up and down the valley. His heart wouldn't have been in it even without Carmen. After all, it was Mora who was the subject of his investigation. His mind was repeatedly drawn to Rancho La Libertad, and, as if pulled by a magnet, he soon found his wagon once again heading up toward that big house on its knoll. The same little band of vaqueros rode up alongside, but this time there were friendly comments from the riders, some of whom he now knew by name. Mora seemed glad enough to see him, although there was a certain constraint in his manner that indicated to Doc that Mora was well aware of the interplay between him and his sister. Carmen, to Doc's surprise, was a little cool. That night after dinner, instead of joining the two men in the study, she excused herself and went off to bed, leaving Doc feeling rather empty.

The next morning, however, she asked him to go riding with her. Since it was daylight and since it was really quite difficult to be truly alone anywhere near the center of the ranch, since a vaquero might ride into view over a hilltop at any moment, Doc felt that it was safe enough to agree.

Carmen was much more vivacious this morning, talking animatedly to Doc as they rode away from the ranch house. They had picked their mounts from among the many horses always kept saddled and bridled near the front door. To Doc's surprise, Carmen rode astride. She was wearing a split skirt. She rode like one of the vaqueros, obviously born to the saddle. Feeling quite sneaky about it, Doc ensured that the horses trotted for a while, just so he could watch the girl's breasts bounce up and down inside her off-the-shoulder, Spanish-style blouse. They bounced very little.

The horses were outfitted with center-fire saddle rigs, what the rest of the country called the California rig, with the latigo more or less in the center so neither the back nor the front of the saddle would lift up under the strain of roping or riding. They were using rather simple saddles today, with only the one leather *michila* in place. The *michila* was an oval leather housing used to cover the wood and leather saddle tree, with cutouts for the horn and the cantle. Doc had also seen some hand-tooled silver-studded *corazas* in the barn. The *corazas* could be used over the *michila* for fancy show, but were heavy for the horses to carry. Doc liked his saddle. It was comfortable and strong. A saddle for living in.

The horses were marvelously well trained to the neck rein. For a half hour Doc was having so much fun that he concentrated more on the riding than on the girl.

However, Carmen soon asked that they stop and dismount. "I have some wine and food," she said, sliding gracefully to the ground. The *michila* of her saddle had over it one of the leather *coronas* used for traveling, with big leather pockets in the front. While Doc was dismounting and tying his horse to a bush—Carmen didn't bother, and her horse seemed happy enough to remain ground-hitched— she took from the pockets of the *corona* a rather substantial meal of bread and cheese and wine and olives and laid it out attractively upon a tablecloth she'd placed on the ground.

They had stopped in a little stand of live oaks. Fallen oak leaves formed a soft, springy mat underfoot. They were prickly little leaves, but there being a thick layer of them, they were comfortable enough to sit on. The day was warm but not hot. Winter was approaching, and the slight breeze had an edge to it; but the trees shut off part of the breeze, while the sun came through a gap in the branches, shining down like a benediction onto where they were sitting. Carmen was charming and unthreatening, and Doc felt relaxed until the wine began to work on him. Then he became intensely aware that he was finally alone with this lovely young woman. She herself seemed totally unconcerned, chatting easily, smiling a little—a warm and somewhat amused smile. He could smell the scent of her; it was a warm, sweet scent.

"Uh . . . perhaps we should get back to the house," Doc said somewhat thickly. "Your brother will worry."

"Why? What could he possibly have to worry about?" Carmen asked. She had been sitting, as he still was, but now she got up onto her knees, very close to him. "You have some oak leaves in your hair," she said matter-of-factly. "Let me take them out for you."

Before he could stop her she had leaned closer and her fingertips were moving through his hair. Her touch was electrifying. The way she was reaching up had pulled her breasts high. They were right in front of his face. He saw the tips of her nipples forming little mounds against the material of her blouse. She was close enough so that he could feel her body heat, and then she sat back on her heels in front of him, a couple of little oak leaves in her hands. "There," she said.

Her face was still very close to his. Her eyes looked enormous, her mouth soft and sweet. Her lips were slightly parted, showing the tips of white, even teeth. She looked straight into his eyes, unsmiling but not exactly serious, and Doc felt his heart stop. Oh God ... here you go, he told himself and was on the verge of reaching for her when he became aware of the sound of several vaqueros passing by outside the oak grove.

That should have broken the spell, but it didn't; it merely postponed it. The tablecloth and the remains of the meal were packed away without a word, and the two of them mounted and rode purposefully toward the ranch house. Something had passed between them during that moment when their faces had been so close, an unspoken promise waiting to be realized. That promise might have faded away had they not, when they reached the ranch house, found Manuel Mora swinging up onto the back of a horse.

"There is a cow with a broken leg on the other side of the ranch," he told them, and was gone, riding off with a half-dozen vaqueros.

The house was empty when they entered. The house staff was down at the stream washing clothes. Not a word was spoken between them. Carmen looked Doc straight in the face, then walked down the hall and into her bedroom. Doc noticed that she did not close the bedroom door behind her. He stood at the head of the hallway, undecided, then slowly started toward her door. When he reached the doorway, he stood just outside it, looking in.

Carmen was slowly undressing. She looked up at him and continued. She had taken off her skirt and was wearing only her blouse and an underskirt. Doc put his hands against the doorframe, waiting. Carmen looked at him again, then with one smooth motion pulled the blouse up over her head and tossed it into a corner. Doc saw her breasts pulled high by the motion. They settled only a little lower as her arms descended. As he had suspected, they were large breasts for such a slender woman and, also as he had suspected, beautifully formed.

He was moving into the room as she bent to slip off her underskirt. She was wearing nothing beneath it, but then, he'd already been certain that would be the case. Carmen was far too much the artist to fumble with anything as prosaic as underdrawers.

She turned toward him now, displaying the dark triangular patch of silky-looking hair at the point where her long lovely legs joined together. Doc stopped, stunned by her loveliness. Seen straight on, her breasts were full and rich, the tips curving up tautly, ending in rose-brown areolae. Those lovely breasts were rising and falling rather quickly now, suggesting the girl was not as cool and collected as she was pretending. In fact, she was beginning to breathe like a steam engine.

The girl strained toward Doc. A low moan of accumulated frustration broke from his lips, and he moved forward to intercept her, dropping to his knees in front of her, his hands, then his lips touching her breasts on his way down. Her breasts were warm, heavy, the tips stiffening quickly as his lips brushed over them. He drew first one nipple, then the other, into his mouth, while his right hand dropped down to the girl's velvety knee, then slid slowly up the smoothness of her inner thigh. He felt Carmen tremble. Her entire body gave a spasmodic shudder when his fingertips moved in between her thighs, sliding slowly into the liquid heat underneath the silky pubic hair.

The rest was a blur, a barely remembered series of wild actions that eventually brought them to her big bed. Both Doc and Carmen tore at his clothes, and within seconds he was as naked as she. Their bodies strained together on the bed, flesh rubbing against flesh, the girl writhing underneath him, every line of her body a silent demand. And then not so silent.

"Please . . . please," she panted. "I can't wait another second. Take me . . . take me . . ."

And then he was inside her, a smooth thrusting into slick heat, clinging flesh, her body surging upward to meet his. No shy, shrinking flower, not this girl. Doc wondered briefly where she'd done this before, and with whom, and then he wasn't thinking anymore, simply moving, following the lead of his body, the girl doing the same beneath him, uttering sharp little cries of obviously overpowering pleasure.

That first mating didn't last very long. The entire preceding week had been one long agonizing foreplay for both of them, and in less than a minute both Doc and Carmen were climaxing, their bodies straining together frantically, hands grasping, moving, sliding over flesh, breath intermingling as they moaned, sighed, and cried out into each other's mouths.

They made love twice more before anyone returned to the house. They had two entire hours together, and in between making love they talked and talked and talked, discovering with unfeigned amazement how much they had in common, how similarly, despite the differences in their ages and backgrounds, their minds worked.

The next few days were a blur of sensuality. Doc and Carmen made love whenever it appeared they would not be discovered, and quite a few times when it appeared probable they might. They made love in the oak grove, they made love in Carmen's room, they made love in Doc's room, with Carmen slipping into his bed, naked, in the middle of the night. They were so overpowered by each other that only a blind man would have failed to guess what was going on, and Manuel Mora was not blind. Several times Doc caught the man looking at him speculatively. He was quite prepared for trouble, but it didn't come. Why not? Doc wondered. Mora was certainly a man who put a lot by appearances, a man of honor, but here Doc was, fucking Mora's sister almost underneath his nose.

But Mora had reasons for holding himself back that Doc was not aware of. Even so, the growing tension might have precipitated trouble if it had not been abruptly broken, or more correctly, rechanneled. The change came when Raider finally showed up at Rancho La Libertad.

CHAPTER SEVEN

The same day that Doc made his initial visit to the Mora rancho, Raider finally rode into the little settlement that lay about seven or eight miles from its front gate. It wasn't much of a settlement: a general store that sold a little of everything, run by a man named Johnson from San Diego; a blacksmith shop; a few run-down frame houses; but, most noticeably, a large rambling structure that served as saloon, restaurant, hotel, and, on occasion, theater. It was owned and run by a fat Californio in his late fifties, known only as Paco. Raider had heard about Paco's place from people he'd talked to on the way inland, and once in the little settlement he rode straight up to it and tied his horse's reins to the hitching rail.

The place was more or less deserted when Raider went inside, just old Paco slowly wiping glasses behind the bar, and a woman straightening up chairs in the back of the room. It was a big room, furnished with rough-cut circular tables and simple chairs, smelling of beer and sawdust and several years accumulation of unwashed bodies. A typical backwoods saloon.

Raider went up to the bar. "Señor?" Paco asked, his deceptively sleepy eyes giving Raider the once-over.

"A beer and a room, if you got one free," Raider drawled.

Paco's right hand automatically grabbed a beer mug while his left opened the tap. "We have a room, señor, but it is not free. Twenty-five cents a day. Plus twenty-five cents for each meal. Fifty cents if you eat a lot."

"I eat a lot."

Raider drained half the mug of beer in one long thirsty gulp, then paid his nickel. He drank another beer before going outside to get his saddlebags and rifle. Paco had already called a stable hand, who was waiting outside, ready to take Raider's horse to a stall.

When Raider went back into the saloon, Paco called out,

"Conchita, show the señor to his room. And be sure you come back."

The woman who had been moving chairs around in the back of the room turned, and even before she fully faced in his direction, Raider knew she was young. She moved young. And despite her shabby clothing, she was a damned fine-looking woman. Raider decided that much after one quick appraisal of the solid breasts filling out the front of her blouse, and the few inches of slim ankle and calf that showed above her shoes. She came closer, moving energetically, and as she moved out of the gloom at the back of the room, Raider saw that she had big dark eyes and a bright, mischievous smile on her pretty mouth.

"*Qué guapo!*" she said appreciatively, as she boldly returned Raider's appraisal, her eyes running up and down his lanky body. "How handsome!"

Paco turned his eyes up toward the ceiling. "Conchita," he said warningly, "Be good . . . and be sure you come right back."

The girl grinned. "Of course. He needs a bath first, anyhow. Would you like me to give you a bath, señor?"

Raider looked quickly at Paco, but he was once again busily polishing glasses. By now the girl had turned and was leading the way to a set of stairs in one of the rear corners of the room. Raider found it easy enough to follow her provocatively swishing hips, and he felt a tightening in his groin. It had been a long time since he'd had a woman, too long, and this girl—he remembered that Paco had called her Conchita—gave the definite impression of being available. He wondered how much she'd charge.

The stairs led to a long narrow hallway with doors spaced evenly along either side. Conchita guided Raider to the last door on the end. There wasn't much of a room on the other side of that doorway, nothing much in it but an old dresser, a water pitcher and basin, and a bed. It was a big bed, though, and looked fairly comfortable.

Conchita stood in the doorway, one hip leaning lazily

against the frame. "There is a bathhouse downstairs, behind the bar," she said.

"And I need it," Raider grunted.

She nodded. "Yes . . . you need it."

"And you'll, uh . . . scrub my back?"

"If you need the help, señor."

She remained leaning against the doorpost, a slight smile tugging at her lips. Raider took a step toward her, and she immediately slipped out into the hallway. "I'll show you where the bathhouse is," she said, already walking down the hallway.

Raider was once again behind those marvelously undulating hips, and, snatching up his saddlebags, which contained a change of clean clothing and his razor, he set off after her.

Conchita led him down another set of stairs and through a door into a large room with a big tin tub in the center. She immediately began to build a fire in a large stove. When the fire was roaring loudly, she placed a large container of water on the stove top to heat. It was a big container. Raider was surprised she lifted it so easily. "You can shave first, if you want," Conchita told him.

Raider was a little uncomfortable. The girl seemed surprisingly matter-of-fact, considering she was in a bathroom with a man. He followed her suggestion, shaving in front of a cracked mirror on a side wall, watching the girl in the mirror as she shoved more wood into the stove. She was a looker, no doubt about that, and about as shy as a mama mountain lion in heat. He knicked his face once, because he was busy watching the girl's big breasts bounce and jiggle inside her blouse as she worked.

He helped her pour the hot water into the tub when it had heated. She was perspiring a little from the heat, her face flushed. His eyes followed a little trickle of sweat as it ran down into her cleavage. She didn't seem to notice. He tore his eyes away and stuck his hand into the water. "Ouch!" he muttered. It was too hot.

Conchita fetched some cold water and poured it into the tub bit by bit, until Raider told her he liked the temperature. He expected her to leave then, but she began refilling the water containers at a pump in the back of the room. "Aren't you going to get in the tub?" she asked, her back turned to him.

He hesitated, then thought, the hell with it, and began taking off his clothes. She turned around just as he was hanging his pants on a nail, totally naked. She took a long, obviously judgmental look at his lean, scarred, powerful body, nodding in approval. "I'm glad you like it," Raider snapped, annoyed.

"Oh, it's very impressive, señor," she replied, and he realized she was looking straight at his crotch.

Raider quickly stepped into the tub and slid most of his body beneath the water. "Do you always stare at naked men?" he asked grumpily. He was accustomed to more retiring women. He was accustomed to being in control.

"Oh, señor, I stare at men with clothes on, too," she said without rancor. "Now I can scrub your back, if you want."

Raider didn't say yes, nor did he say no. The heat of the water was wonderful, already cooking the trail-ache out of his muscles. He sank down a little lower into the tub as the girl came over to him, a long-handled brush in one hand, a bar of soap in the other.

"Lean forward," she said, soaping the brush.

He thought, What the hell? and did as she asked, and a moment later she was indeed scrubbing his back, standing to one side of him as she worked the brush. She was bent forward at the waist. He found himself looking down her blouse as gravity pulled it away from her body, a pair of nature's finest only inches from his eyes, two big breasts swooping outward from the girl's body, jiggling a little as she scrubbed his back, but obviously nice and solid. He caught a glimpse of first one nipple, then the other, and then this nice little tableau disappeared as the girl straightened up and handed him the brush.

"I think you can handle the rest, señor," she said.

The girl was about to turn away when Raider reached out and took her by the arm, drawing her toward him. He tried to draw her down so that he could kiss her, but she easily slipped out of his grasp; her arm was slippery with soap.

"The service includes only the bath, señor," she said matter-of-factly.

"Damn it, you prick-teaser," Raider said angrily.

Now the girl grew angry. "I do as I wish, señor," she snapped. "No man can make me do otherwise."

Raider had half stood up, and suddenly the girl was laughing. He saw where she was looking and realized he had an erection. He immediately sat back down in the water. When he looked up again, he saw that Conchita was no longer angry. "You are right," she said. "I was teasing you. I have been cruel."

"Goddamn right," he said sulkily.

"I'm not always cruel," she said. "I can be . . . never mind."

She turned to go.

"Hey . . . wait!" Raider protested, standing up again, sloshing water onto the floor. At the sound of his voice she turned back to look at him, once again straight at his crotch. He still had the erection.

"I was right, señor," she said, grinning. "It is very, very impressive."

And then she was gone. Raider sat back down in the tub. "Now don't that beat all," he said wonderingly.

CHAPTER EIGHT

An hour later Raider was eating his supper downstairs in the saloon—a big slab of roast beef cooked in a spicy sauce, along with beans and tortillas. Damned good food, he decided. He had long ago gotten over his aversion to chili peppers, and like so many who had grown accustomed to Mexican food, he was hooked.

Conchita had served him the supper and, according to Paco, had cooked it too. She was bustling about as if nothing had happened between them in the bathroom, and Raider figured, in a way, that was how it really was—nothing much had happened. Just one hell of a peculiar girl.

He was dipping a tortilla into the last of the spicy meat sauce when suddenly there was a commotion outside, the thunder of hooves, the squeal of excited horses, the wild yelling of men. Raider let his tortilla fall into his plate and, backing his chair against the wall, laid his hand on the butt of his revolver.

"It is nothing, señor,' Paco said. "Just the vaqueros from Rancho La Libertad coming in to have a little fun. It is Saturday night, you know."

So it was. "Rancho La Libertad?" Raider asked.

"Yes. Manuel Mora's rancho."

Raider moved his hand away from his pistol but kept his chair against the back wall. Mora's crew. That was a stroke of luck. They were coming to him.

A moment later the door to the saloon burst open and men started pouring in. A wild-looking bunch, Raider decided, but wild in a cheerful way. They all wore vaquero garb: flaring trousers, tight vests, bright sashes filled with knives, and big sombreros. There were more than a dozen, bellying up to the bar, ordering something to drink, some yelling at Conchita to bring food. Their manner showed that they considered Paco's place their place. Home. Raider wondered how they would take to his presence here in their living room.

They were only now beginning to notice him. A slight hush fell over the proceedings. There was a whispered conversation between Paco and a stocky, powerful-looking man a little older than most of the other vaqueros. Paco nodded, and some of the tension went out of the men.

The stocky one came over toward Raider. Without waiting for an invitation, he pulled up a chair and sat down on the opposite side of the table. Raider, once again munching his tortilla, looked at the man, waiting. "I am told you speak Spanish, señor," the newcomer said.

Raider nodded. It was true. He had been speaking Spanish ever since he'd arrived at Paco's. It had come a little hard at first, but the more he spoke, the more his Spanish came back.

"Drink with me," the man said, looking straight into Raider's eyes.

Raider knew what was coming. The testing. The machismo game. The proof of manhood so important to Latin males. To males of other cultures, too, but they were often less forthright about it.

Raider signaled Conchita, meaning to ask her to bring a bottle and two glasses, but she had already anticipated him, and the glasses and the bottle were on the way. She put them down on the tabletop. The newcomer's arm went around her waist as she stood beside him, his hand sliding down onto her buttocks. She smoothly turned away, leaving the hand in empty air. The man grinned after her as she walked back to the bar, then he turned to Raider, who was pouring whiskey into the glasses.

"I am Diego, *capataz* of the best rancho in this valley," he said proudly.

So, Raider thought. This was Mora's *capataz*, his foreman. A good man to cultivate. He'd have to be careful not to kill him if he got out of line. Raider introduced himself. Glasses were raised. They were big glasses, and under the unspoken rules of the machismo game, both men poured the entire glassful of rotgut straight down their throats. As soon as the liquid hit Raider's stomach, he wanted to vomit, but he fought it back. The empty glasses hit the table. Raider did his best to make certain that his face did not give away the fact that his insulted stomach was still heaving.

"Ah . . . good," Diego said, but Raider had noticed that tightening of the other man's mouth that suggested the whiskey had been no kinder to Diego's stomach. He managed a bright smile nevertheless. "What brings you to our valley, Señor Raider?" he asked.

"Oh . . . just passing through. Working a little here, a little there. Drifting, really."

"You a stockman? You work with the animals?"

Raider shrugged. "I've been known to. Done a little mining, too. Whatever brings in the beans."

The conversation went back and forth in this manner for quite some time, to the accompaniment of more of the awful whiskey. Raider thought longingly of the wonderful stuff he'd had on the train. Everybody in the saloon was drinking, the vaqueros laughing and joking and playing pranks on one another. Some of them were throwing knives at a wall across from Raider and Diego, aiming at knots in the wood.

Diego turned around and looked proudly at his men. "They are good, are they not?" he said.

It was said like a challenge. Raider, his head a little mushy from the booze, shrugged, then, seeing an opening in the crowd between him and the wall, he suddenly reached down and, drawing his bowie from its sheath, threw it in one smooth, glittering motion. The big knife flashed past the knife throwers, glittering in the light of the kerosene lanterns, startling some of the men before burying its point right in the center of a knot.

There was an immediate uproar from the vaqueros. *"Madre de Dios!"* one exclaimed. "And from a chair!"

"Very impressive," Diego said. Raider nodded modestly, not bothering to mention that he had been aiming for another knot. He might not have tried it if he hadn't been a little drunk. He'd gambled, and it had paid off. There was no mistaking the admiration in Diego's eyes. The *capataz* turned and bellowed to Conchita for another bottle of whiskey, much to the alarm of Raider's perennialy queasy stomach. The girl came walking toward them, her hips performing that disturbing swing that had been bothering Raider ever since he'd first seen the girl move. When she put the bottle on the table, Diego's arm went around her again, his hand lightly massaging the rounded swell of her buttocks.

She smiled down at him. "If you do that any more, Diego, I will cut off your hand."

It was said in such a normal tone that Raider was not sure he'd correctly understood the words until he saw first shock, then anger on Diego's face. Here comes trouble, he thought, but the girl turned coolly away, and after a moment's internal struggle, Diego chose to laugh. "A very unusual woman," he said to Raider.

"So I've noticed."

Diego grinned, his pride saved. "Ah, you too, then? She makes one think that . . . and then . . . Well, in her case, one can understand."

Obviously a story was about to be told. Raider waited without prompting, and Diego began to speak. "She was the only daughter of a poor family, up from Sonora," he said. "Her father was a drunk and her mother a nothing. It's hard to believe that such a beautiful girl could have come from such garbage. And that she survived. You see, from a very early age she had a cunt that itched day and night, and being a person of strong will, she made sure her cunt got what it wanted. When she was barely a girl, she was sneaking out of her father's miserable shack as many nights as she could, making the beast with two backs with whatever man she chose.

"And she chose. That's the important word. She would not let any man touch her unless it was her idea first. Her father found out. Word gets around when that kind of thing happens. He beat her to make her stop, and then, when he saw that it would do no good, the bastard thought he would try to get some for himself. Imagine, señor! From his own daughter!

"But that was *his* mistake. She was a big girl by then, and she took a knife to the old sot. Came close to cutting his balls off, from what I've heard. She moved out on her own after that, earning her bread however she could, and, surprisingly, spending less time with men. Only once in a while, and then only with men she herself chose—at least, until a little while after she began working for Paco. One night a group of drunken saddle tramps came through. Three of them. They dragged her into the bushes and raped her. But they made an even bigger mistake than her father— they did not kill her. She came back later that night with a shotgun and blew them to pieces around their own campfire. Since then, few try to force our Conchita."

Raider nodded. A real strange one, that girl. It was social suicide for a young woman to run around openly taking lovers. She'd never be able to marry. Maybe she didn't want to. Maybe she'd just spend the rest of her life working in places like Paco's, fourteen hours a day. Sure could cook.

The night became more of a blur as the whiskey continued to flow. Diego challenged Raider to arm wrestle. Raider had decided to do his best not to beat the smaller man, at least not too badly, but to his surprise, he had to struggle not to be beaten. Finally, both panting, they declared it a draw. Most of the other vaqueros were warming up to Raider, impressed not only by his knife throwing, but also by his willingness to join in with their fun. There was only one man who held back, a lean, mean-looking customer named Pedro. He had started the evening glaring at Raider, and as he drank more and more, he became vocal, his insults growing louder and louder until Raider could no longer ignore them.

Pedro was sitting only a few feet away. Raider turned to face him. Suddenly the room was very quiet. Another test of machismo on its way. Pedro was slumped forward a little, a half-empty glass in one hand, his mean little eyes glaring at Raider, a nasty sneer on his thin lips.

Raider smiled. "You open your mouth one more time, pilgrim," he said softly, "and I'll help you close it."

He did not know how the others would take this. Pedro was, after all, one of them, although Raider had noticed that Pedro did not seem all that popular with the other vaqueros. Another gamble, and now the call.

Pedro's sneer broadened. "Gringo pig..." he started to say, but Raider was on his feet instantly, lunging toward Pedro. Pedro tried to get up, the whiskey spilling from his glass, but Raider was already on him, picking him up by the front of his dirty embroidered vest, careful that the other man's hand didn't stray toward his knife, but Pedro was too surprised.

Holding the vaquero in front of him like a doll, Raider marched toward the front door. Laughing, someone opened it, and Raider threw Pedro out into the night. The vaquero's boot heels came down hard on the wooden veranda, and he tried to regain his balance, but he was moving backward too fast, and with a yell he fell onto the dirt next to the hitching rail. He lay there, blinking, then, screaming with rage, he leaped to his feet and charged Raider, reaching for his knife.

Raider, instead of backing away from the knife, once again rushed the man, pinioning Pedro's knife arm with his left hand while he sank his right into Pedro's stomach. Pedro's breath whooshed out in an agonized gasp, and, as he doubled up, Raider easily took away his knife. He threw the knife far into the darkness, then grabbed Pedro by the scruff of the neck and deposited him in the watering trough. Raider stood over his man and said quietly, "If you get out of there before I get back inside the bar, vulture-vomit, I'm gonna get real mad."

He'd said it in English, but there was no mistaking the tone of his voice. Pedro appeared to understand, because he remained in the water, his eyes glaring hatred, while Raider walked calmly back into the saloon. The other vaqueros were silent, standing around in a big circle. Raider was beginning to think he had made a mistake, until Diego broke the tension by saying, "It is good that you did not really hurt him. Pedro is a pig when he drinks, we all know that, but when there is bloodshed, it is bad. Always bad."

The festivities soon started up again, and Raider knew he had gained another notch upward in the respect of the vaqueros. However, it was not over yet. Raider was standing at the bar with Diego when Pedro came crashing in through the door, his face twisted with hate. "Now you die!" he screamed at Raider, his right hand going for the butt of the big old cavalry six-shooter he had stuck in his belt.

Men scattered from the line of fire, but there was no fire. Raider, charging forward again, moved in on Pedro before he could bring his pistol up. Raider's own pistol was in his fist, appearing as if by magic. He lashed the heavy barrel across Pedro's face. Blood spurted, and the man reeled back, his old pistol discharging a ball into the ceiling. He was falling now, and before he could get off another shot, Raider plucked the pistol from his hand.

Pedro lay on his back, blinking dazedly, blood running from the cut Raider's revolver barrel had made across his forehead. Raider stood over him, his Remington aimed down at the other man's face. There was dead silence in the room as Raider thumbed the hammer back. The sound was awful in that silence. "If I ever see you again, you son of a bitch," he grated, "if I ever see anything except your back goin' in the other direction, and goin' fast, then I'm gonna blow your fuckin' head off. Understand?"

Once again he'd spoken in English, and once again the message was clear.

"Understand?"

Pedro, staring up into the awesome black hole in the muzzle of Raider's .44, knowing that a few ounces of pressure on the trigger was enough to kill him, nodded quickly.

"On your feet!" Raider snapped, lowering the hammer. Pedro scrambled sideways, trying to make distance, then staggered upright. One last glance back at Raider, and then he was running out into the night. A moment later, the sound of a horse being run hard, and only then did people start breathing again.

Diego, face serious, came up to Raider as the big Pinkerton holstered his .44. "He will go away for now," he said. "But it is not over."

"What do you mean?"

"He will leave the ranch. He will be too ashamed to face the rest of us after his humiliation. He has been shamed, and that is why he will be back. For you, Raider. *La venganza*. Vengeance. To regain his manhood. His shame must be washed away in blood, even if he has to shoot you in the back from ambush."

Raider snorted, still angry. "He'll have to stand in line."

"You are good with that gun? You can shoot, as well as hit a man in the head with it?"

There was a certain edge to Diego's voice. Raider realized that he had distanced the man a little, distanced all of them. By shaming one of them, even one as unpopular as Pedro, he had shamed them all a little. He thought quickly, looking for a way to win them back. "Yes," he said abruptly. "I can use the damned thing."

He had two of the men line up six candles on a bench against one wall. Six lighted candles, the flames rising from them straight and clear. Standing a dozen feet away, his hands hooked lazily in the front of his gunbelt, Raider let the tension build, then, when he sensed it to be at its peak, he suddenly drew the big Remington, leveled it at the candles, and tore off six quick shots.

The heavy report of the .44 reverberated deafeningly inside the room. A dense cloud of gunsmoke hung in front of Raider as he began rapidly reloading his pistol, and one of the men laughed, because all of the candles were still upright. Then someone else shouted out the obvious. Not one of the candles was still lighted. Raider had shot out the candle flames without moving the candles.

Jubilation. Any hostility was forgotten. The vaqueros loved a show. Indeed, Raider's treatment of Pedro had been ennobled by his performance. He could obviously have killed the man if he'd wanted, but he hadn't.

"Ay! Qué macho!" Diego shouted, slapping Raider on the back, causing him to drop one of his cartridges. "More whiskey!" he bellowed at Conchita.

The whiskey was brought. Toasts were drunk, an outwardly happy occasion, but Raider remembered that he was going to have to watch his back, going to have to keep an eye out for Pedro for as long as he was in these parts.

There was the sudden sound of hoofbeats outside. Raider wondered if Pedro was bringing in reinforcements, but when the saloon door crashed open, there were only another two wild-eyed vaqueros. *"Un oso! Un oso grande!"* one of them shouted. "Killed a cow up by the mountains only a few hours ago."

Diego pounded Raider on the back again. *"Qué bueno!"* he laughed. "A grizzly, attacking our cattle. Wonderful!"

"That's *good?*"

"Of course, señor," Diego roared. "We will go hunt him in the morning."

CHAPTER NINE

Raider felt like hell. If only he'd been able to get a couple of hours' sleep, but no, here he was, dawn still an hour or so away, on his horse, riding along with a bunch of crazy vaqueros who were laughing and cutting up as if they'd just had ten hours in bed.

At least he was out of that damned saloon with its stink of cheap whiskey. Raider gagged as he thought of the huge amount of panther piss he'd poured down along with the others. When his stomach didn't remind him what an idiot he'd been, his head did.

However, the fresh air was rapidly clearing his brain. Fresh, hell . . . it was damned chilly. It obviously got *cold* in California. He wished he had his heavy sheepskin jacket, instead of the leather one. The vaqueros, however, seemed comfortable enough in their heavy serapes. Not a bad idea, the serape, he thought. Just a blanket, really, with a hole cut out for the head.

It was beginning to get light. A faint glow was forming around the top of the huge mountain that loomed above them. Raider hoped the whole damned thing would be over with quickly. He'd shoot the bear, then hightail it back to Paco's for a few hours of shut-eye. There was no doubt he was going to have to be the one to do it. Not one of the vaqueros had a rifle. A few had old pistols, but a pistol wasn't going to stop a grizzly. No way. Raider had had the foresight to beg the loan of an old Sharps .50-caliber buffalo gun that Paco had hanging behind the bar. Paco had requested his Winchester as a guarantee that the Sharps would come back home. Raider had been happy enough to agree. Even his Winchester .44-.40, with its hard-hitting cartridge, was awfully light to bring down a full-grown grizzly. They took some real killing. What the hell did these vaqueros think they were doing, riding out after such a monster without any real hardware?

75

Oddly enough, Diego had been equally concerned when Raider insisted on taking his own horse. "Perhaps you would like one of ours," he had said. "The sight of the bear . . . the smell . . ."

"I've seen bears before. So's the horse," Raider replied testily. He didn't need any advice from this bunch of obvious amateurs.

The light grew slowly, picking out clumps of brush and a few trees down by a streambed. Raider could now see that the mountain above them was heavily forested in pine and fir. Palomar Mountain, Diego had called it. They were riding along its base. "Rancho La Libertad is only a couple of miles over that way," Diego told him, pointing down into the valley. "I hope the bear is close. It would make everything that much easier."

What the hell was he talking about? Raider wondered. Afraid of being away from home?

One of the riders spotted the bear shortly before sunrise. Raider rode over the top of a little rise, and sure enough, there it was, still wandering near the carcass of the cow it had killed, obviously getting ready for breakfast. Raider spotted the dark forms of a couple of coyotes lurking nearby in the brush, waiting for a chance at the meat if Papa Grizzly got careless.

He was definitely a male. Even at this distance Raider was impressed by the size of the big silvertip. Obviously the bear hadn't seen them yet. Raider slipped the big Sharps out of his saddle scabbard and was looking for the best way to get a little closer when Diego rode up, his face anxious. "We will not need the gun, señor."

"Yeah? What the hell are you going to do, then?" Raider demanded, his aching head making him touchy. "Throw rocks?"

"The *reata,* señor. We want him alive." He hefted the long rawhide lariat attached, coiled, to his saddle.

"Take him *alive?*" Raider demanded, gaping incredulously. He lapsed into English. "You gotta be outta your cotton-pickin' *mind!*"

"The *reata larga* is all we have ever needed," Diego replied, laughing. Already a number of the others were shaking out their lariats, testing the thin, flexible, incredibly strong ropes. Each one had been handmade out of intricately braided hide. Raider watched as one rider took out after a running jackrabbit. To Raider's amazement, the vaquero threw his loop from at least forty feet away. More amazing yet, the loop fell right onto the rabbit. The rabbit was caught for a moment but was too light to pull the loop completely closed. There was a frantic struggle, dust flying, the rope tautening, finally falling slack, the rabbit racing madly away, zigzagging for all it was worth. A laugh from the vaqueros and then all at once the entire pack of them thundered over the ridgetop and raced down toward the bear.

"*Vamanos!*" Diego shouted to Raider, who, rather reluctantly, dashed off after the others.

The coyotes heard them coming first and melted away into the brush. Old Papa Bear, starting to feed on his malodorous breakfast, looked up once, took another bite, and only when it was clear that the riders were coming straight at him did he finally show signs of annoyance. Grumbling, he stood up on his hind legs, showing a mouthful of truly awesome teeth.

Raider knew that the bear's real weapons were the terrible nine-inch claws on the ends of those powerful paws. One blow from either the left or the right was easily capable of disemboweling a man or a horse, even of breaking a steer's neck.

The bear stood its ground for a moment. To a grizzly fifty or sixty years before, when they had known only poorly armed Indians from whom they had little to fear, man had been merely a curious annoyance. However, the coming of the Europeans, with their guns and their daring, had made Papa Grizzly and all his kin stand up and pay attention when the hated man-smell came their way.

The bear turned and began to shamble away, turning back once as if it meant to try a last mouthful of cow. But the riders were too close. The bear gave up and headed for a thicket about a hundred yards away. Four riders raced ahead of the rest and cut him off. The bear made a rush at one of the horses. The horse merely danced out of the way. Raider's own horse, as Diego had feared, was by now half mad from the bear's smell, much less the sight of it. Raider tried to get the horse to run in with the others, but it fought the bit and spurs, trying to turn and head in the opposite direction.

Raider saw the first reata thrown, a truly amazing cast, the huge loop sailing far through the air and settling accurately around the grizzly's thick neck. The reata jerked taut, the vaquero snubbing the loose end around his saddle horn. The bear pulled away for a moment, then, with a thunderous roar, charged the horse and rider who had caught it . . .

Only to have another loop thrown around its neck from the other side, then a third snaking onto its left hind leg.

The bear fell full length, one leg pulled out straight behind it, and now the riders with their reatas around the bear's neck backed their horses away, exerting tension on their lines. The loops tightened, and Raider could hear the bear gasping for breath. In a few seconds its eyes were bulging and its wild struggles diminished.

With the bear down and quieter, Raider was able to get his horse under at least a small measure of control. He rode up beside Diego, who was watching the proceedings from a small knoll about fifty yards from the captured bear. "Is that it?" Raider asked. "You just choke the damned thing to death?"

Diego shrugged. "It has been done. Normally, if we want to kill it, some of the men go in with their knives."

Raider shuddered. The thought of going close enough to a grizzly to stab it . . . If one of the reatas were to break under the enormous strain . . .

"But this one we will take back with us," Diego said.

Raider cocked a disbelieving eye. "Oh, really? And how are you going to do that? Saddle him, put a bit in his mouth, and ride him home?"

"Ah, Raider, you have no faith. Look! There goes Arturo now."

One of the vaqueros had ridden close in front of the bear and was throwing sticks at its nose. The nooses around the bear's neck were loosened. Raider could hear air whooshing back into the animal's lungs. It began to get its strength back and a moment later managed to struggle up onto all four feet. Raider's blood turned cold. Arturo and his mount were damned close. One good rush from the bear and . . .

That's exactly what happened. The bear, bellowing in anger, charged forward, straight toward Arturo. Raider was amazed that the vaquero was able to keep his horse under such good control. Horses have a well-founded fear of grizzlies, but Arturo's horse let the bear get amazingly close before finally pirouetting away. Too late, though. Raider knew the bear would easily be able to run the horse down before it stretched out into a run; but then the vaquero with the leg rope snubbed his line tight, and the bear flopped down on its belly again, its trapped leg stretched out behind it. Once again the loops tightened around its neck, choking it into submission.

But ground had been gained. The bear's mad rush had carried it a good twenty-five yards—in the direction the men wanted it to go. The operation was repeated again and again, first one man then another teasing the bear until it charged, the men with the reatas bringing it to a stop when it threatened to get out of control.

The bear's bellows of rage turned into roars of maddened frustration. On occasion the vaqueros were able to trot the confused animal along like a big dog on the end of a leash. Then the bear would collect itself and try and kill the nearest man or horse. One time the leg reata broke and the bear began fighting madly against the lines around its throat. Raider saw the horses thrown off balance by the terrible power of the huge animal. It might have broken loose if a vaquero had not dabbed another string onto its other hind leg.

It was still morning when they got the bear to Rancho La Libertad. Fortunately, it had been a matter of only a couple of miles over relatively easy country. Raider, awed by the riding and roping ability of his former drinking companions, watched them herd the bear into a cage built into the wall of an oval log stackade. Only then were the loops shaken loose and the big door allowed to drop into place. The bear roared and fought, slamming his massive paws against the rough wood imprisoning him, but there was no way out. Finally he slumped down, panting, his little eyes glaring madly at the puny creatures standing, laughing, just the other side of the bars.

Now that the bear was safely put away, Raider took a look around him. So this was the place Maximilian's gold had bought. Nice-looking spread, and Jesus, one *hell* of a good-looking woman coming out of the big ranch house. Followed by two men, unfortunately, one dressed in the stylish garb of a rich Mexican, the other one some little American dude . . . Doc!

Raider kept his face from showing any recognition. Doc and the Moras, had, of course, been drawn out of the house by the roaring of the bear. Diego introduced Raider to Mora and his sister; Mora introduced Raider to Doc.

"Any friend of Diego's is always welcome at this ranch," Mora said to Raider. "Perhaps you already know—the men are having a fiesta today. No special occasion, but then, they seldom need an excuse to celebrate. I hope you will stay."

Raider voiced his acceptance, but his eyes rested much longer on Carmen than on her brother. Up close she was even more of a looker. He wondered if . . . no, she was standing awful close to Doc, that sneaky little bastard.

Diego pulled him away. "Now we will have some fun," he said.

"Like what?" Raider grumbled. "We gonna try stuffing mountain lions into gunny sacks?"

"Oh no, just a few games. But first . . . some meat."

Raider drifted along after Diego, trying not to be too

obvious as he cast a couple of long looks back at Carmen.

"She is very beautiful, is she not?" Diego chuckled. "She is something all of us dream about, but I think that the little gringo has beaten us there. Ah . . . the cow."

For a second Raider thought Diego was making a slighting comment about Carmen, but then he saw that a cow was being trotted out into an open area. A couple of mounted vaqueros began herding it back and forth, whacking it with the ends of their reatas, thoroughly rattling the animal.

"Our dinner," Diego said.

Raider wondered what the hell they were doing with this walking meal, when the cow suddenly bolted between the horses of its two tormentors and headed away in a straight line toward apparent freedom. The riders yipped excitedly and took out after it. Raider expected them to drop their incredible loops over its horns, but to his surprise one of the vaqueros drew a long slim knife from his sash and rode up alongside the running cow. The vaquero leaned over and drove the knife's point straight down against the back of the cow's neck, severing the spinal cord. The cow, instantly dead, went down like a sack of cement, ass over horns, in an ungainly tangle of flying legs. The vaquero's horse danced nimbly away from the cartwheeling corpse. Other vaqueros immediately dabbed loops onto the animal's hind legs and dragged it toward a semi-outdoor kitchen where others waited with skinning knives.

The man who had killed the cow came trotting over, grinning. Raider saw that he was not one of the men who had been at Paco's place. Despite the riding skill he'd just shown, on closer inspection he appeared quite old, at least seventy. But goddamn, Raider thought, the man rides like a boy.

"A good *nuqueo*, Tiberio," Diego said to the old man.

Tiberio's bright old eyes sparkled. "Ah, *señor capataz*, it brings back the old days."

"Tiberio was one of the best of the *nuqueadores*," Diego said to Raider. Then, seeing the look of incomprehension in Raider's eyes, he added, "A *nuqueador* is one who stabs the animal in the back of the neck, the *nuca*. Tiberio could not tell you how many times he has done that."

"True, señor," Tiberio sighed nostalgically. "In the old days, before the *Yanquis* came to stay for good, we in California did not have much—only our animals and what the land could produce. The winds made sailing up from Mexico very difficult. There was no steamship then, and from time to time the Yuma Indians turned against us and closed the route across the Colorado from Sonora.

"I lived on the rancho of my uncle, along with my family. Our wealth consisted of our herds; even a poor man might have cattle. Yes, we had all those animals and nothing to do with them, and then the Boston ships came and wanted the hides. How that changed our lives! We had wealth! Now when a ship arrived we would herd the cattle to the *matanza*, the killing ground, and kill thousands, usually with the *nuqueo*. Then the *peladores* would strip the hide from the carcass, the *tasajeros* would cut up the meat for jerky or salt beef, and the women would cut the fat and tallow away and take it to the rendering vats and later put the rendered tallow into big sacks made out of green hides, to be dragged to the coast and taken out to the ships. Ah, those ships, señor! Once, when I was a boy, my uncle took me aboard one. We rowed out through the surf. I was certain we would drown, but we made it. Once aboard, I could not believe the wealth there—tools, good cloth for clothing, candlesticks, tableware, all the things we had never had in the old days. And we could have them all now because of our cattle."

The old man obviously wanted to relive more of the old days, but Diego was anxious to join the younger men in a little fun. Raider had noticed that they were burying a squawking rooster in a little hole in the ground, until only his head stuck out. "The *carrera del gallo*," Diego said.

The riders leaped onto their horses. One of them thundered down toward the rooster. The bird's head swiveled frantically, his beady little eyes trying to look in every direction at once. The rider bent far down from the saddle, his hand reaching for the rooster's head . . . and he missed.

Hoots and catcalls from the other riders. The one who had missed rode away shamefaced. Already another was pounding toward the rooster, leaning, his hand reaching, and he rode away triumphant, holding the flapping rooster high for all to see.

Diego gave Raider a sideways glance. "Would you like to try it?" he asked innocently.

Several vaqueros were standing near, all of them pretending not to listen, but Raider knew that they were. They were testing him again. Damn! He'd have to do it. Thank God they weren't asking him to do something really hard, like maybe housebreak a bull moose. He mounted, cursing inwardly, already seeing himself falling out of the saddle and landing on his head.

If he'd been watching a little more closely, he would have seen that the men burying his rooster had big grins on their faces. What Raider didn't know was that they were burying this one extra deep, tamping the earth tightly around it.

Raider began his ride. His heart was in his mouth as he leaned down, his right hand groping for that elusively weaving chicken head. At the last moment he saw how solidly it was buried, but too late to change his mind. The bird's head was in his hand and he tugged hard as his horse raced along, feeling the resistance, sensing that he was going to fall after all. The weight of the bird was dragging him down. No, I don't want to fall, he thought frantically, and put out an extra effort, drawing himself upward, and all at once he was erect in the saddle, saved, his hand full of an amazingly light rooster, then, to his disgust he saw that he was holding only the bloody head. A glance backward and he saw that the rest of the rooster's body was still firmly in the ground.

He rode up to Diego and tossed him the bloody chicken head. Diego neatly sidestepped. "Well, one for the pot," Diego said cheerfully, pointing to where some of the vaqueros were digging up the decapitated chicken. Then he smiled and gave Raider the ultimate compliment. "You ride like a Californio, gringo."

The day continued in a seemingly endless round of macho competition, most of it on horseback, all of which Raider wisely kept away from. The butchered cow carcass was turning slowly on a spit over a huge bed of coals, beans were being cooked, tortillas patted into shape. And then, the day's main event.

The grizzly.

Doc walked up to Raider. "I've been told we're about to have a bear and bull baiting," Doc said. "I never have liked that particular sport."

Raider looked past Doc, toward Carmen. "Some piece, Mora's sister. Gettin' some o' that, Doc?"

Doc's face tightened. "You keep your filthy mouth off her," he said tersely.

"Uh-huh. So that's the way it is."

But Doc had already turned away, walking back toward the Moras. Raider looked at the girl, then met Mora's eyes. Mora was looking at him very hard; then he turned away and led Doc and his sister toward the enclosure where the bear was being kept. Others began to follow. Raider went along with Diego and the vaqueros.

Crude bench seats had been built above the palisade wall, giving those seated there a clear view into the enclosure. Everyone took a seat.

A roar from the bear. Someone had managed to get a length of chain around one of its hind legs. The chain trailed out under the cage door. There was a commotion in a stall next to the bear's cage. A man passed the other end of the chain into the stall. More commotion, and then, to the delighted cheers of the onlookers, the cage and stall doors were opened simultaneously. The bear hesitated, confused by all the shouting, but a huge black bull came bursting out of the stall and ran into the arena—until brought up short by the chain that anchored it to the bear.

That was enough for the bear. It came shambling out into

the open, tugging with its leg at the chain. The bull pawed the ground, snorting, and then made a halfhearted pass at the bear. The bear raked the bull's back with its claws, opening long bloody furrows.

Enraged, the bull charged again, this time straight on. The grizzly reared up on its hind legs and with one powerful swipe of its right paw broke the bull's neck.

It was over that fast. The bull dropped, motionless, still attached to the bear by the chain. The bear, roaring with rage, jerked at the chain, bloodying its own leg, but the chain tore through the flesh and bone of the bull's leg and came loose.

The bear was free inside the enclosure. It lumbered from wall to wall, looking for a way out, stretching upward, but its mighty claws were not quite able to reach the top. Raider felt sorry for the animal, trapped, maddened, degraded. In the open, in the wild, it had exhibited a savage nobility. Raider remembered the way it had looked—free, arrogant, the massive head high, the dark body hair tipped with silver.

Doc, too, felt pity for the animal. He glanced quickly at Carmen. She had obviously been entranced by the clash between the bull and the bear. There were still spots of color high on her cheeks. Her breasts were rising and falling rapidly. She looked back at him, and he saw how much she wanted him, how much the spectacle in the arena had aroused her in all ways.

Someone now turned another bull into the enclosure. It ran back and forth, obviously wanting nothing more than to get out of there. But the bear had seen it now and, maddened, raced toward the bull on all fours. The bull danced out of the way, then ran, the bear charging after it, raking it once on the rump, and now the bull too became angry. It raced the length of the arena, turned, and charged straight at the bear. Up came the grizzly onto its hind legs, huge paw high for the kill, coming down, thwacking against the bull's body, but too late. One of the bull's long horns had sunk far into its belly. The bull continued to drive forward, grinding the horn in deeper. The bear screamed in pain, trying to back off that terrible horn. One more frantic swipe of the paw and the bull's neck was broken, the animal falling, its blood-streaked horn sliding out of the bear's belly.

The bear rolled over and over, biting at its stomach, howling, then began to race around the arena, frantically trying to get away from the pain, but the pain followed. Slowly the bear weakened, finally sitting down and pressing its paws to the bleeding hole. A shiver of morbid excitement passed through the crowd. Doc glanced at Carmen again. She was leaning forward in her seat, her eyes glittering, her breathing shallow. Doc remembered the girl in bed. Yes, the same signs.

Suddenly the booming report of a heavy-caliber gun startled everyone. A puff of dust jumped from the bear's hide, right over the heart. The animal reared upward one last time, stood wavering on shaky legs, then fell over backwards, dead.

Doc turned. Raider was standing on one of the seats, a smoking Sharps rifle in his hands, looking down at the bear. Then he turned and left. A sigh passed through the audience.

Doc nodded to himself. "I owe you one, Raider," he murmured.

CHAPTER TEN

Raider's unexpected shooting of the bear had cast a pall of uneasiness over the festivities, but the natural high spirits of the Californios could not be kept down for long. By now the meat was cooked, the feast prepared. Raider was invited to sit down with the men at long tables made of rough-hewn wood. At least two pounds of barbecued meat was placed in front of him, along with beans, tortillas, corn, tomatoes. He ate it all. The men around him laughed, shouted, drank, ate. Two of them almost got into a knife fight, but public pressure immediately restored peace, and in a few minutes the would-be combatants were once again laughing and joking together.

The Moras and Doc were eating at another table a short distance away. Raider looked over once and caught all three of them looking his way: Doc, pensively; Mora, with an expression Raider could not fathom; and to his surprise Carmen was sending his way a mixture of belligerence and intense interest.

Despite being offered a place to sleep, Raider insisted on riding back to Paco's. He didn't want to give the Moras a chance to ask him too many questions. He did find time to exchange a few words in private with Doc. Neither man could say they had accomplished much, but both were in position if anything happened.

A small band of vaqueros came for Raider. Despite his half-hearted protests, they insisted on escorting him back to Paco's. They brought with them, of course, as many bottles of wine and other firewater as they could carry, and by the time Raider finally sighted Paco's place, he was reeling in the saddle. Assured that he had reached his goal, the vaqueros wheeled their horses and galloped away, yipping exuberantly, apparently as fresh as when they had shown up at Paco's the night before.

Raider staggered inside, through the bar, up the stairs,

and into his room. The bed drew him, but first he made sure of his security as much as was possible. The door did not have a lock. The best he could do was stack a couple of glasses on the floor against the inside of the door. Then, off with his clothes and into the bed.

For the next several hours the only sound in the room was that of his regular breathing. Then, in the very early hours of the morning, the faint creak of footsteps outside his door. The doorknob turned very slowly. The door began to open. Raider's survival sense had him awake even before the glasses toppled onto the floor. His right hand disappeared beneath his pillow and reappeared holding his .44. The hammer clicked back just as a shadowy form slipped in through the doorway.

"Don't shoot!" a soft voice whispered.

It was Conchita. No mistaking the voice. Raider slowly let the hammer down, aware now of the soft glow of flesh. The girl was naked!

The Remington went back underneath the pillow as Conchita slipped into bed with him. The heat of her flesh shocked Raider. He reached for her, his hands exploring the softness of her breasts.

"I want you," Conchita murmured.

"Sure as hell looks that way," Raider replied, his hands slipping further down her body. Her flesh was soft, silky, hot. The cleft between her thighs was all of the above, plus very, very wet. Yes, she obviously wanted him, and her body'd had time to work on the idea.

There was little speech, just the soft rustle of sheets, the sibilant sound of flesh against flesh, an occasional sharp intake of breath when contact was made with something particularly sensitive, then, as Raider rolled over on top of the girl, a whimper as he drove into her, a whimper that soon rose in volume.

Conchita was obviously no inexperienced virgin. She moved languorously under Raider, her hands kneading his back muscles, slipping down to his buttocks, pulling him more deeply into her. As his own passion mounted, as he swelled inside her, his hardness increasing, his climax only seconds away, her body exploded into motion, bucking, writhing, driving up against his, her half-muted cries sighing into his ears, and then he was coming with her, gasping, moaning.

They collapsed together, their bodies wet against each other, their breathing slowing bit by bit. Raider rolled free and was about to ask Conchita a question, but she glided smoothly from the bed. She stood quietly for a moment, looking down at him. The moon was shining in through the window, silvering her body, outlining the full thrust of her breasts, the shaded convexities and concavities of her waist, hips, and thighs. Her beauty was so overpowering that Raider was unable to speak, and then she was heading for the door, moving easily, her body still exhibiting the graceful sensuality Raider had just experienced with his own body.

"*Hasta luego*," she said softly, and then she was gone.

"Goddamn," Raider muttered, a little groggy. Well, at least she'd said, "*Hasta luego*." Until later. A promise? He sure as hell hoped so. Then, with a satisfied if somewhat wistful smile, he fell asleep, not bothering to restack the glasses against the door.

He slept late, missing his breakfast, but made it downstairs in time for lunch. Conchita brought him his meal, her manner matter-of-fact, all business. It was as if the night before had never happened. "Well, if that's the way she wants it," Raider muttered. She was the same for the rest of the day, and by evening Raider was beginning to wonder if it *had* really happened.

She came to him again that night. He was half waiting for her, not hoping too much, but he felt a gladness when she once again slipped in through his door, her naked flesh glowing softly in the dim light. Once again they made love without speaking. When it was over, Raider expected her to leave again, but to his surprise she became talkative.

"I told you I wanted you," she said.

"Guess so," he replied laconically.

"I wanted you from the first day I saw you, but you were

too sure of yourself, too *machisto*."

He said nothing.

"I am not a nun, you know," she said with a surprising amount of fervor.

"Not hardly."

"Some of the men call me a *puta*, a whore," she said bitterly. "Because I do as they do—I take what I want. They do not call *themselves* whores."

"Next time one of them does, you just let me know," Raider growled. He was confused by her words. After all, nice girls didn't go around sneaking into strangers' beds.

"I do not need anyone's protection," she said fiercely. Then her voice softened. "I don't ask money from men," she said. "I ask only that we give one another pleasure, and that the pleasure is given freely, without force or trickery. Is that so wrong?"

"Hell, no," Raider replied uneasily, wondering what the hell she was getting at.

Now she seemed to be talking half to herself. "I have always . . . wanted," she said somewhat sadly. "Even when I was very young, when we lived in the country. When I watched a bull mount a cow, or a ram chase a ewe, and heard the ewe bleat with pleasure when the ram caught her, something seemed to happen inside my body, way down . . . here," she said, her hand gliding down over her belly. "I had so much time to myself. My father and mother were too drunk to . . . but that is not important. I simply decided to try those things I had watched other creatures do, those things that excited me so much. I did try them. And I have been doing them ever since."

"Ever thought of getting married?" Raider asked.

"And have a man own me the way my father owned my mother?" she said with revulsion.

"It don't always happen that way."

She shook her head sadly. "There is always ownership."

There was enough moonlight for Raider to see the sadness on her face. Then, as if realizing she had let him see too far into her, she suddenly smiled. "I . . . am wanting it again," she said, her voice becoming husky. She rolled toward Raider, her body radiating heat and desire.

Well, honey, you came to the right place, he thought, and gave her what she wanted.

But he did not completely forget the things she had said, even if he did not quite understand them. The next day he watched her as she bustled about the saloon and kitchen. A real strange one, he thought. But one hell of a fine person. Too bad Doc wasn't here. He'd understand. He always understood things like that.

Raider hoped she'd slip into his room again that night. She was making the waiting here easy, but he sure as hell wasn't getting anywhere on the case. Just marking time. Maybe he should find a way to set himself up out at Mora's ranch, ask for a job. He could slip out to Paco's at night for Conchita.

Raider's thoughts were interrupted by the sound of horses being pulled up in front of the saloon. He thought it might be some of the local vaqueros, then decided that this group was too quiet. A moment later the front door of the saloon opened and in came some of the hardest-looking men Raider had seen in a long time. Gringos. Gunfighter trash. The man in the lead, big, if not quite as big as Raider, lean, fast-looking, appeared to be a little more intelligent than his companions, who were a scurvy-looking crew. There were seven of them in all. They fanned out from the door, quickly scanning their surroundings for possible surprises, in the manner of men who live with sudden death, then they moved over and sat down around two tables, their backs against a windowless wall.

They had, of course, seen Raider. The leader's eyes rested speculatively on him. Raider's table was only a couple of yards away. The newcomer nodded. Raider nodded back. "Name's Logan," the stranger said. "Jake Logan, from Arkansas way."

"Placed your talk," Raider replied. "Name's Raider. Fulton County's where I got my start."

Now that it had been established that they were both

Arkies, Logan seemed to warm up a little, the way a shark might warm up at the sight of something swimming by. "Been around these parts long?" he asked.

"Few days. How 'bout you?"

Logan shook his head. "Jus' passin' through. Got some business here. Lookin' for a man named Mora. Manuel Mora. Ain't run across him, have you?"

Deadpan, Raider replied, "Think I've heard the name. You might do better to ask the locals."

Logan nodded but said nothing further. Raider noticed that old Paco, who had obviously overheard everything, and probably had enough English to have understood about Mora, was polishing glasses more briskly than usual. The men with Logan, after beating trail dust out of their clothes, were now showing signs of thirst.

"Hey!" one of them, a squat, ugly man, shouted at Paco. "Whatta we gotta do to get some drinks around here?"

"Maybe you could learn the lingo first," Logan said, then motioned to Paco. "Something to drink, hombre," he said in passable Spanish.

Paco came around the bar, a bottle of whiskey in each hand. He called out toward the kitchen, but Conchita was already on the way, balancing a stack of glasses.

"Well, looky here," the squat man said, leering at Conchita. "Nicer piece o' tail than you'd 'spect to find in a dump like this."

"Shut up, Brewster," Logan said quietly. Brewster flushed and started to reply, but Logan stared him down. Raider suspected that it would be a full-time job running herd on this bunch of cutthroats, but he also suspected that Logan might be the man to do it. He had a cold, speculative deadliness about him that already had Raider watching his every move.

The men began drinking heavily, pouring Paco's rotgut down their throats like it was beer. Raider noticed that Logan drank very little, sipping slowly, his eyes continually traversing the room. Raider doubted a cockroach could sneak up on him. He was looking at Paco, and Raider knew he was going to ask him about Mora and wondered what it was all about. He didn't think Logan intended a simple friendly visit. It had to be something to do with the gold.

Suddenly there was once again the sound of horses outside. One of Logan's hardcases quickly got to his feet and peered out one of the little windows in the front of the saloon. "Hey, Jake," he said. "It's those Mexes again. The ones we been seein' all the way from Arizona."

Logan seemed to tense a little. So did his men. All of them moved their chairs back more tightly against the wall, their eyes turning toward the door. It opened, and a dozen Mexicans filed inside. Not vaqueros, not quite bandits. As hard a group as Logan's, every man armed to the teeth, pistols on their hips, ammunition belts crossed over their chests, knives in their belts. Raider caught a glimpse of at least one man still outside, guarding the horses. A bunch of professionals.

The Mexicans fanned out in a semicircle, facing Logan's men without being overtly hostile about it. The one Raider took to be their leader, a heavily mustached man in his middle thirties, medium-sized, lean, put his back against the bar and unerringly picked out Logan as the leader of the seven gringos. "Señor," he said, nodding politely.

Paco began to move more quickly than Raider had yet seen him move, bringing whiskey and beer for the Mexicans. Conchita brought glasses. Several of the Mexicans grinned at her but made no rude comments. A real disciplined bunch, Raider thought.

"Name's Logan," Jake said to the Mexican. He said it in English, and the Mexican replied passably well in the same language. "Gutierrez. From . . . Sonora. Your health, señor."

Gutierrez raised his glass, drank. Logan did the same. Raider, seated somewhat out of the center of things, held his peace. Gutierrez turned around, although his men continued to face Logan's men, obviously guarding Gutierrez's back. Gutierrez called Paco over and began speaking rapidly in Spanish, some of which Raider missed, but he understood enough to realize that Gutierrez, too, was asking about Mora. Paco stammered, hesitating to say anything, but he also obviously did not want to antagonize Gutierrez. Gutierrez, realizing Paco was holding something back, frowned, leaning toward Paco.

Then Logan broke in. "Seems like we're both lookin' for the same man."

Gutierrez turned around, looking at Logan even more carefully than before. "Ah . . . then we have, how do you say, a coincidence?" he said softly.

For the time being both men left Paco alone. Raider suspected that neither Gutierrez nor Logan wanted to press the matter. Neither wanted the other to find out where Mora was. It was, for the time being, a standoff, with the two leaders continuing to face one another, sipping slowly at their drinks.

Some of Logan's men, however, were belting down the booze as if they were afraid they'd never see anything like it again. Brewster, the squat, ugly man who'd been so interested in Conchita, was drinking particularly heavily, his little pig eyes never leaving the girl. With so many men in the saloon, she had a great deal to do, bringing mugs of beer, bottles, food for those who were hungry. Brewster's head swiveled back and forth on his thick neck as he watched her.

Then a new factor added itself to the potential flash point of this volatile situation. The door opened again and in came Pedro, the man Raider had pistol-whipped a few days before. He was armed, an old pistol thrust into his belt. He swaggered inside, his eyes darting from left to right, finally settling on Raider. His mouth moved into what he probably intended to be a sneer, but Raider could see the fear in it. He suspected that the only reason Pedro'd had the guts to come into the saloon was because of the large number of horses outside, probably figuring that the sheer press of numbers would keep Raider off his back. Not that Raider minded. As far as he was concerned the trouble had ended the other night—if Pedro wanted to leave it that way.

Pedro gave Gutierrez's cold stare a wide berth. Gutierrez had read him straight off. Logan was friendlier, perhaps because he had also read Pedro straight away and figured he might be of some use.

"Come on over and have a drink, amigo," Logan said.

Pedro, glancing quickly at Raider, sat down in the chair Logan had pulled out for him, on the opposite side of the table, so that Pedro was facing Logan and his men, his back to Gutierrez at the bar.

Logan began to warm up Pedro, plying him with whiskey. Raider suspected Logan was about to ask him about Mora. Gutierrez must have suspected the same thing, because he motioned Paco over, ready to pump him about Mora while Logan was busy with Pedro.

Then, an interruption. Conchita, bringing beer for two of Logan's men, passed close to Brewster. He reached out a big hand, pressing it against her body, across the groin. "When you git finished, honey," he said, "you come on back here an' sit yourself down with a real man."

Conchita stiffened, then hissed something in Spanish. Brewster's face tightened. "What the hell'd you say?" he demanded, squinting up at the girl.

"She call you a son of a peeg, señor," Pedro cut in, turning toward Brewster.

"Why you..." Brewster snarled at Conchita, coming partway out of his chair. Raider also started up from his chair, his face tight. Pedro noticed, and immediately suspected what the girl was to Raider. Talking to Brewster but grinning at Raider, he said, "She is only a *puta*, señor, a whore. Any man's woman—if he is man enough to take her."

Brewster leered up at Conchita, his eyes raking upward from her hips, over her breasts, finally resting on her face. "I reckon I'm that man," he chuckled, and once again his hand went out, his thick fingers cupping around one of Conchita's breasts.

"*Mierda!*" she snarled, and hit Brewster on the side of the head with one of the full beer mugs.

The blow knocked Brewster back. The beer drenched him. "Fuckin' whore!" he bellowed and, lunging forward, hit Conchita on the side of the head, knocking her to the floor.

Several things happened at once. "Brewster!" Logan shouted, but he was too late. Raider had already covered the distance between himself and Brewster, and smashed his fist into the other man's face. Brewster got his legs tangled up in a chair and fell over backward. Men scattered, Pedro lunging around behind Raider.

"Watch out!" Raider heard Conchita shout, and an instant later Raider heard the sound of a gun hammer being cocked behind him.

There was no time to think; he was suddenly spinning to his right, sidestepping, his right hand scooping his .44 out of its holster, and even as he spun he was aware that Brewster, still flat on his back, was going for his own gun.

When Raider had turned far enough he saw that Pedro had his cocked pistol aimed straight at him, but Raider was already slipping to his own right. By the time Pedro fired it was too late to correct his aim. He fired straight at where Raider had been a split second before, and missed, his bullet slamming into the wall. And now Raider's pistol was coming up, the hammer cocked, the muzzle aligning itself on Pedro. Raider saw the man's eyes widen in fear, saw his thumb fumbling frantically with the hammer of his pistol, trying to cock it again, but Raider put a bullet into the center of Pedro's chest, knocking him backward. Raider watched him slam into the bar and start to fall, but Raider was already continuing the turning motion to his right, once again sidestepping, facing the wall, catching Brewster in the act of aiming, and as the man tried to correct his aim and track after Raider, Raider fired, trying for Brewster's chest, but not quite making it, the shot going higher, tearing through Brewster's thick neck. Brewster jerked, his pistol firing, the shot going harmlessly into the ceiling, and then he was thrashing on the floor, his hand tearing at his throat as he strangled on his own blood.

Raider immediately backed away, keeping his pistol high, warily watching the rest of Logan's crew. Most of them had been caught with drinks in their hands, and it had all been over so quickly, first Pedro, then one of their own.

They sat, tense, obviously ready to make their moves, but Logan bellowed, "The first man who goes for his iron gets mine across the top of his head."

That doesn't fit the man, Raider thought, and then he saw the reason for Logan's caution. Gutierrez's men, already more or less fanned out around Logan's, had their hands on their gun butts. Two more were standing halfway inside the front door, rifles ready. Logan's men saw this too, and not a person inside the saloon dared move. A classic stand-off.

It was Gutierrez who broke the ensuing silence. "I think it is time we all left," he said softly. His eyes never leaving Logan, he laid money on the bar behind him. "For the drinks," he said to Paco. Raider noticed that it was a gold coin.

Gutierrez's men slowly filed out of the bar, the two riflemen by the door standing guard. By the time the last of them had left, Raider had moved to the back of the room conveniently close to the rear door, his pistol still in his hand. Conchita was nowhere in sight. Paco was still behind the bar, both his hands below it. Raider figured he was holding a gun.

Logan quickly sized up the situation. "Come on, boys," he said to his men, getting slowly to his feet, his right hand well away from the butt of his revolver. "Time to hit the road."

"But," one of them snarled, glaring at Raider, "Brewster ... We can't just—"

"Sure we can," Logan snapped. "He was stupid, and he's where stupid people end up—dead. Now, let's us smart people get our asses outside."

Cursing, the other five trooped out of the bar. Logan remained behind for a moment, looking coldly at Raider. "Damned good work with that iron," he finally said. "'Specially against two backshooters. But you owe me a man, mister, and someday I'm gonna collect."

And then he too was gone, coolly turning his back on Raider and walking out the door.

CHAPTER ELEVEN

Raider was reloading the Remington's two empty cylinders when Conchita burst in through the rear door, carrying the big Sharps he had used to kill the bear.

"They're gone," he told her.

She looked around the room, saw that he was right, all gone—except for the bodies of Pedro and Brewster. Paco had come around the bar and was looking down at Pedro.

"I sure as hell hate to leave you two with this mess," Raider said curtly, "but I've got to get out to Mora's and tell him about Logan and Gutierrez."

Conchita nodded. Raider went up to his room, collected his gear, then went out to the stables and began saddling his horse. He had just thrown the saddle over the animal's back when he heard the quick pounding of a horses's hooves outside, but by the time he'd gotten to the stable door, whoever was riding that horse was out of sight.

Raider mounted and rode out into the yard. Conchita was standing on the front veranda of the saloon, looking up at him. He waved. She didn't wave back, just continued to watch him as he trotted his horse out of the yard and onto the main trail.

Raider had gone over a mile before he realized he wasn't absolutely sure just where Mora's ranch was. The only times he'd traversed the route, he'd either been hung over or drunk. He took one wrong turn before he finally felt he was on the right path.

He arrived at Rancho La Libertad in the middle of the day. There were few vaqueros moving about; Raider suspected most of them were enjoying their siesta.

The sound of his horse brought Diego outside. "Ah, Raider," he said, looking somewhat surprised.

Raider quickly looked around him. No one else in sight. "Is the little gringo doctor here?" he asked.

Diego looked at him speculatively. "Yes, in the house. I will take you to him."

Diego led the way inside the big house. Raider was relieved that they met no one inside; he was not yet ready to talk to Mora. Diego led him to a door, knocked on it, then turned and walked off when Doc answered from within, "Yes?"

"It's me. Raider. Let me in."

The door opened. Raider quickly stepped inside past Doc. "Close the door," Raider said. "We got trouble. There's all kinds of people runnin' around these parts lookin' for Mora."

"Yes, I know. So does Mora."

"How the hell . . . ?"

"A rider came in just a little while ago. I overheard him talking to Mora. Mora's pretty upset."

Raider remembered the sound of a horse racing away from Paco's place. That must be how Mora knew. "Hell, Doc, maybe this is our break," Raider said tersely. "Mora's gonna be spooked. Maybe he'll deal with us now that those varmints are after him. Lemme tell you, I sure as hell wouldn't want 'em after *me*."

"I don't know if we should unmask ourselves," Doc said dubiously. Raider could tell there was something bothering him, and he had a suspicion of what it was. He was about to speak when the door opened and Mora himself walked in, followed by Carmen.

"Ah, Señor Raider," Mora said cooly. "I had been told you'd arrived."

He looked from Doc to Raider and back to Doc again. "Would I be mistaken in assuming that you two already knew one another before coming here?"

"Well, sure," Raider said. "We've met before. Why, back in Colorado, when I was feelin' poorly . . ."

"And would I also be correct in assuming that neither of you is what you appear to be?" Mora continued somewhat more acerbically.

"I . . ." Raider started to say.

"Shut up, Raider," Doc said. He faced Mora. "Yes, you're quite right," he said, his face expressionless. "We're here about the gold. At present we represent the bank to whom it lawfully belongs."

"Ah, that miserable gold," Mora said bitterly. "I wish I had never seen it."

"You have it, then?" Doc asked, but Carmen suddenly stepped forward and slapped him across the face. "You . . . miserable . . ." she said bitterly. "You used me. You made a mockery of me."

"No, it wasn't that way. Not with you," Doc insisted, but Carmen's expression was icy.

"I despise you," she said in a strangled voice, turning away and walking out into the hall.

Doc started after her, but Mora held up his hand. "I prefer that you leave my sister alone," he said coldly.

Doc said nothing, but Raider burst out, "Let's stop all this playacting. Things are heating up. There are men runnin' around this neck of the woods lookin' for you, Mora, an' I don't hardly think they want to dance."

"I know. I heard. I also know that you killed one of them, along with one of my vaqueros."

"*Your* vaquero? That skunk was gonna sell you out."

"And you *haven't?*" Mora retorted sharply. He visibly brought himself under control. "But, tell me about these men," he finally said.

Raider shrugged. "There's a bunch of hardcases led by a man named Jake Logan. Ever hear of him?"

Mora shook his head.

"And a bunch of gunslingers up from Mexico. Led by someone called Gutierrez."

Mora paled. "Gutierrez!" he burst out. "Valdez's man!"

"You know him, then?"

"Yes," Mora admitted. "I know him. Ah," he said sadly, "they have found me now."

"He's after you 'cause o' the gold, isn't he?" Raider demanded.

"Yes, the gold," Mora said lifelessly. "That accursed

gold. I should have known I couldn't run away from it."
He squared his shoulders. "It is time I brought this to an
end," he said briskly. "I will go and see Gutierrez . . . offer
him all that I have. Anything that will make him leave this
place alone . . . and the people in it."

He had glanced at Carmen, who was standing stiffly in
the hallway, her back to them. He turned back to Raider.
"Diego tells me that about a dozen men are camping not
far from the ranch. It must be Gutierrez. I'll go see him
now."

"Take plenty of men," Raider said.

"No. I'll go alone."

"That's loco!" Raider burst out. "That Gutierrez is one
hell of a dangerous hombre. And Logan's still runnin' around
loose somewhere out there. If you go alone . . ."

"No," Mora repeated. "I will not involve anyone else in
this. It was my error to begin with, so it is I myself who
must set it right. I will not risk the life of even one of my
men."

"At least take us with you," Raider insisted. "It's our
job."

Mora looked scornfully at both Raider and Doc. "You
would be the last I would take," he said. "Spies . . ."

He called out Diego's name. The *capataz* appeared in
the doorway with two other men. All three were armed with
old single-shot rifles. Raider sensed movement at the
window and, turning, saw that another two men were leaning on the window frame, pointing pistols at himself and
Doc.

"You two will wait here until I return," Mora said. "I
will deal with you later."

"Hell, maybe you ain't *gonna* return," Raider said angrily. "Don't go runnin' off half-cocked."

Mora looked at him pityingly. "When I return we will
have a little talk about honor, and what it means to a man
of breeding."

Raider saw Doc flinch, then Mora turned and walked out

the door. Raider started to follow, but Diego raised his old rifle and pointed it straight at Raider's chest. There was no friendliness showing on Diego's face. Raider relaxed and stepped back. A moment or two later there was the sound of a horse galloping away from the hacienda.

"The damn fool," Raider snarled.

"He is a man of honor, señor," Diego said hotly.

"Honor? Shit! He's gone off to get himself killed, and he knows it. Is that what you want? Is that what you all want?" he shouted at Carmen's back.

She turned around, her face white and strained. "Do you really believe that is what will happen?" she asked. She was speaking only to Raider, carefully avoiding looking at Doc. Doc himself was facing half away, staring straight at the wall. Raider felt sorry for him, but there was work to do. "Yeah," Raider growled. "I met this Gutierrez. He ain't no sweet little ole lady wantin' to help out. I don't know if you know anything about this gold, but right now there's one hell of a lot of people around here who want it, including the people who hired us, and I can promise, you, lady, we're the only ones that are even a little bit friendly."

Indecision played over Carmen's lovely features. She looked despairingly at Doc. He felt her eyes and turned to face her. "Do you think . . . ?" she managed to ask him.

Doc nodded. "I've never know Raider to make a mistake about trouble. If he says your brother is riding into danger, then that's the way it is."

Carmen abruptly made up her mind. "Diego," she snapped. "Get all the men together. Make certain that everyone is armed."

"But señorita Carmen," he protested. "Don Manuel said that we must—"

"Don't argue with me!" she said sternly. "My brother's life is in danger. If we stay here and let him die . . ."

Diego nodded. Motioning to the guards, he led them from the room. In a matter of seconds there was a great deal of shouting outside, followed a few minutes later by the sound of horses neighing and the clink of equipment.

"Come on, let's get our asses movin'," Raider growled, starting out of the room.

Doc started to follow, stopping for a moment next to Carmen. He looked into her face. Her eyes met his for a moment, then she quickly looked away. Doc turned and followed Raider.

Outside, Doc went to his wagon for his shotgun, while Raider untied his horse from the hitching rail, and another for Doc. Vaqueros were still pouring out of the bunkhouses, carrying a bizarre assortment of old and new weapons. Within five minutes they were all mounted, ready to ride, and then there was a cry from the house and Carmen came running out, booted and dressed for the trail.

"I'm coming with you," she said flatly.

Raider wasn't about to waste time arguing with her. "Let's go!" he called out, and with Diego leading the way, they thundered out of the yard, over twenty men and one woman.

Raider was doubtful about the odds twenty normal peaceful vaqueros would have against Gutierrez's well-armed and ruthless bunch, but they were better than nothing. If Mora were killed, they'd probably *never* find the gold.

One of the vaqueros showed them the way to where the strangers were said to be camped. The ride took less than an hour. When they were near, Raider insisted that they slow down and proceed cautiously. He figured that their only hope was to take Gutierrez by surprise. He wondered if that was possible. Gutierrez was good. He'd probably post scouts around the camp perimeter.

But they did take them by surprise. Moving on foot up a small rise, Raider dropped down onto his belly and peered cautiously around a bush. Below, about a hundred yards away, was a small depression, and in it were Gutierrez and his men. And Mora. He must have arrived only a short time before; he was still sitting his horse, looking down at Gutierrez, who was on foot. Gutierrez's men were spread out in a circle around Mora's horse, pinning him in, and even at this distance Raider could see they were grim-faced.

He couldn't hear what Mora and Gutierrez were saying, but he could tell that both of them were beginning to shout. Finally, Mora tried to turn his horse around and leave, but one of the men seized his horse's reins. The animal reared, and another man reached up and pulled Mora from the saddle. Mora hit the ground, rolled once, then sprang to his feet. Raider saw the flash of knives and wished he had Paco's Sharps. He was about ready to order the vaqueros to charge down into the little depression no matter what, even at the risk of Mora being hit in a crossfire, when, to his relief, he saw Gutierrez push Mora away from his men and force his back against a rock.

Doc and Diego had moved up beside Raider. Raider saw Diego go rigid with anger when he saw how his *patrón* was being treated. Raider laid a restraining hand on the *capataz*'s shoulder. "Tell the men that we'll have to surround that bunch. Once we get around them . . . Oh, shit, what now?"

A small group of mounted men had suddenly appeared on the skyline, on the opposite side of the little depression from where Raider and the vaqueros were hidden. Raider strained for a moment to see who it was. "Logan!" he finally burst out.

One of Gutierrez's men had seen them too. He called out, and Gutierrez's people all spun around.

"Hello the camp!" Logan sang out. Gutierrez stepped forward, looking up at the newcomers. Logan called out again, "Kinda looks to me like you got what we want."

Gutierrez's men were scrambling into defensive positions behind rocks and clumps of brush. "Perhaps I do have what you want, whoever you are," Gutierrez shouted back. "But I am used to keeping what I have."

"Now don't go getting all excited," Logan replied. "Maybe we can make some kind of deal."

Raider was trying to decide what to do next, when Diego suddenly acted. "They are looking the other way," he hissed. "Now is our chance."

"No!" Raider said, but it was too late. Diego vaulted onto the back of his horse, and with a wild shout, pounded over the crest of the rise and down the slope beyond, calling for the vaqueros to follow him.

They did. One second they were sprawled on the ground, the next they were in the saddle, racing after Diego. Raider saw Gutierrez spin around. Logan, on his hilltop, automatically pulled his men back a few yards. There was confusion among Gutierrez's men as they scrambled into new positions to meet this sudden threat from the opposite direction.

Mora chose this moment to make his break. He was onto his horse's back in one smooth movement, the animal already running by the time Mora had settled firmly into the saddle. Raider watched Mora jump the animal over some low brush. He also saw Gutierrez bringing up his rifle, aiming at the fleeing man.

Raider swore, tried a snap shot at Gutierrez, missed, heard Gutierrez's rifle boom, saw Mora, who had straightened up in the saddle after his horse's leap, arch backward, sway, nearly fall, then catch his balance and continue on, lying flat along the horse's neck.

Carmen screamed. Gunfire broke out from the charging vaqueros. One of Gutierrez's men fell, then all of them were leaping aboard their horses, dragging the wounded man with them, while firing back at the vaqueros. A horse went down in front of the vaqueros' charge, tangling up some of the animals behind it, and then Gutierrez's men were pounding away.

Diego swerved the men away from pursuit, racing his horse after Mora's. The horse was trotting now, Mora still slumped over its neck. Diego rode up to the animal, caught the slack reins. He shouted something, and the rest of the vaqueros came pounding over.

Raider stayed on the hilltop, watching Logan's men across the way. They continued to sit their horses quietly for another few seconds. Raider stood up. Logan saw him and waved mockingly. It was too far to make out Logan's facial expression accurately. Pretty damned far for a shot, too,

Raider thought, and then it was too late anyhow. Logan signaled his men, and they trooped away in the direction Gutierrez had taken.

Raider mounted and, with Doc following, rode after Diego and the vaqueros. Diego had stopped Mora's horse by taking hold of the reins; Mora was slumped motionless over the horse's neck, the fingers of both hands twisted into the mane. As he rode closer, Raider could see the dark red stain slowly spreading over the back of Mora's coat, right between the shoulder blades.

Doc immediately took charge. "Get him off the horse," he said to Diego. Everyone could hear Mora's gasp of pain as he was lowered to the ground and placed as gently as possible face down on a thick pile of the vaqueros' serapes. Doc quickly cut away the material of Mora's coat. There was a bluish hole in his back slowly welling blood. "Thank God it isn't bleeding more," Doc muttered as he sponged away some of the blood with his handkerchief. "But we've got to get him to a doctor."

"But you are a doctor, señor," Diego insisted.

"Not the right kind for a wound like this. At the very least we've got to get him back to the ranch and into bed. Look. There's no exit wound. The bullet's still inside. It has to come out."

Carmen had now ridden up. She looked down at her brother, ashen-faced. "Oh, my God," she said in a low voice. "Is he . . ."

Doc turned toward her, his face grim. "He's in bad shape. Very bad shape. It's difficult to tell just where the bullet is. They don't always travel in a straight line once they're inside, but from the entrance wound, I'd say it was dangerously near the heart. By some miracle it's missed his lungs. The wound's not sucking air. But if we don't get that bullet out . . ."

Diego sent men back to the ranch for a wagon to transport Mora home. Two other men were sent galloping toward the small village of Escondido to see if they could find the local doctor, but it would be hours before they could reach there and return. Meanwhile, Doc bandaged the wound as well as he could, using strips cut from Carmen's petticoats.

Mora appeared to be only half conscious during the operation, but once bandaged, with the wound protected and the blood flowing less quickly, he seemed to regain his senses. "Let me lie on my back," he half whispered. "I . . . can't breathe."

They carefully rolled him over. Doc didn't think it mattered anyhow. Few people recovered from a wound like Mora's. When Mora looked up, he saw his death in Doc's eyes. "Ah," he murmured. "To come to this." Then he looked around him, at what he could see of his land. "But there are worse places to die."

"Manuel! Don't talk like that!" Carmen burst out.

Mora didn't reply, just looked again at his land. "The gold bought this for me. The gold killed me," he said. "It has killed so many."

His eyes caught Doc's. "I might as well tell you about it now . . . perhaps if only to spare Carmen your further questions when . . . when I am no longer here to speak."

And so, slowly dying from Gutierrez's bullet inside his chest, Manuel Mora told Doc and Raider the story of Maximilian's gold.

CHAPTER TWELVE

Teniente Manuel Mora tensely sat his horse outside the Mexico City branch of the British Imperial Bank of London, watching the last of the mules being loaded. Five hundred thousand pounds sterling, over half a ton of gold coin, was being distributed among four of the mules. The other two mules would be carrying supplies for the journey. Mora sat at attention in his saddle as the commander of the expedition, Captain Count Kodosczy of the Emperor's Hungarian Cavalry cantered toward him.

"Are your men ready, Lieutenant Mora?" Kodosczy asked.

Mora threw the captain a parade-ground salute, which he knew would please the spit-and-polish Hungarian. And why not please him? Mora thought, since he would soon enough be betraying the man.

Mora did not feel good about that. Betrayal was alien to his sense of honor, but he had his orders. More orders than anyone knew. He sincerely admired Count Kodosczy, but there was no getting around the fact that the man was an enemy. An enemy of Mexico.

And what am I? Mora wondered. At present he held a commission as a lieutenant in the army corps of General Leonardo Márquez. Now *there* was a traitor, fighting against his own countrymen for a foreign despot—as I appear to be, Mora thought bitterly.

Four years before, in 1863, after eighteen months of fierce fighting, invading French and Austrian troops sent by Napoleon the Third, Emperor of the French, had finally broken the last active Mexican resistance and forced on the Mexican people, as Emperor of Mexico, that simple-witted dreamer, Archduke Maximilian of Austria-Hungary.

But the French and Austrians had been premature. All resistance had not been crushed, only bruised. After a short breathing space, resistance flared again. Juárez, rightful president of Mexico, had managed to flee to the United

109

States. That great military hero, General Porfirio Díaz, a man whom Mora revered, had escaped from captivity to lead the fight against the French. Now there is a man, Mora thought. He wished he could be fighting alongside his hero. Six months earlier Díaz had defeated Márquez's traitor army—including the Hungarian Cavalry—at La Carbonera, opening the road to Mexico City. And only a few days ago Díaz had liberated Puebla after bloody fighting. Ah, to have been there and to have shared in his country's victories!

But circumstances had dictated otherwise. Manuel's father, a highly conservative aristocrat, a pillar of the Church—which had backed the French-Austrian rape of Mexico—had insisted that Manuel enter the service of the new emperor. Without his father's knowledge, Manuel had immediately slipped out of the capital and offered his services to Porfirio Díaz, but Díaz, to Manuel's surprise and disappointment, had insisted that Mora appear to go along with his father's wishes. "You will be our eyes and ears from within Márquez's camp," Díaz had said.

Despite his bitter disappointment, Mora had been unable to say no to his hero. He had duly accepted his appointment. His father, wishing to keep his only son out of combat, had pulled strings and gotten Mora appointed to Márquez's staff, which was why he now found himself involved in this distasteful undertaking.

The end of Imperial Mexico was clearly imminent. In addition to Díaz's brilliant victories, President Juárez, advancing south from the United States border at the head of an army, had already taken Cuernavaca. There was little left to the Imperialists. Díaz was marching on Mexico City itself, while the Emperor had managed to get himself bottled up at Querétaro, besieged by the Republican General Escobedo, an ex-muleteer. There was little doubt that the siege would be successful at any time and that Maximilian would be either dead or a captive. Time had run out for the would-be Emperor, his imperium collapsing, his wife, the Empress Carlotta, back in Europe, reportedly mad as a hatter, the entire country in chaos, with Maximilian's former allies scrambling to save what they could for themselves.

Which brought Mora back to the work at hand. The gold. Maximilian had ordered a forced loan of the money only two months before, but it had never actually left the vaults of the English bank. Márquez, knowing the game was up, coveted that gold. Facing defeat and possible exile, a golden nest egg is always desirable. The English owners of the bank, likewise seeing anarchy and defeat coming closer and closer, and knowing that their former support of the usurper Emperor would hardly endear them to the eventual victors, had offered Márquez a large bribe to supply them with a military escort that would guard the gold to Veracruz, where it would be put onto an English ship and repatriated to England. What they did not know was that Márquez, while accepting the bribe, had given direct orders to Mora to see that the gold did not make it to Veracruz. To Márquez, the English bribe was merely icing on the cake. He wanted the whole cake. But there were things that even Márquez did not know.

The last of the mules were loaded. Kodosczy gave Mora the order to form up the escort. There were thirty men— ten Mexican cavalrymen and twenty Hungarian lancers. Hardly an army, but speed was to be their main weapon. Speed and surprise. They would dash to the coast before Díaz's army drew its cordon too tightly around the city.

The little cavalcade set out, the Mexican troopers bringing up the rear, the mules in the center, the Hungarians riding two abreast in front. The lancers made a splendid show in their beautiful uniforms: shining gold braid, burnished metal, gaily tossing helmet plumes. Pennons fluttered from the long ash-wood lances, with their sharp, glittering steel tips. They were the cream of Europe's military might. How, then, had they been beaten so many times by rag-tag armies of Mexican patriots?

Captain Count Kodosczy, riding at the head of his little command, had personal experience of some of those defeats. He himself had fought as La Carbonera, against Díaz. How ridiculous the ill-armed Mexicans had seemed to him and to his aristocratic fellow officers when they had first arrived in Mexico. But no longer. Kodosczy shuddered as he remembered the butchery at La Carbonera, the Mexicans refusing to acknowledge that they were beaten, the Mexican cavalry charging, driving back the lancers, a hand-to-hand struggle following, ragged unarmed Indians pulling the guns from the hands of the enemy, the ugly sound of machetes meeting flesh, the screams of horses and men.

It had seemed such an unlikely outcome before the battle, those lines of ragged peasants dressed in what appeared to be white pajamas and little straw hats, Díaz himself wearing a gray cutaway coat. An obvious rabble pitted against crack European troops—those neat uniforms, the truncated conical visors with the suncloths hanging down the back, protecting necks against the fierce Mexican sun, their modern arms. Glimpses of pink faces and brush-cut blond hair as some of the Hungarian officers prepared to put their helmets on before the battle. It should have been so easy to smash that dark-skinned rabble, to prove the white man supreme once again. But those damnable machetes, the Indians strangling his men with their bare hands . . . How he wanted out of this terrible country, with its endless violence and endemic corruption. Of course, it never occurred to Kodosczy that there was an element of corruption in the very fact of being here as an invader in someone else's land.

They had ridden only a few hours when Mora galloped his horse up alongside Kodosczy's. Kodosczy returned the Mexican lieutenant's salute. He liked and respected Mora and could not understand why a man of his obvious honor was not fighting with the Republicans. But why look a gift horse in the mouth?

"Captain," Mora said. "There is something I should tell you.'

Kodosczy listened, his mouth falling open in surprise as Mora told him of the ambush waiting just a few miles ahead. An ambush ordered by General Márquez. "As soon as the trap is sprung," Mora said without inflection, "I am ordered to shoot you in the back."

"But of course, as a man of honor, you cannot do that," Kodosczy said.

"No, sir, I cannot," Mora replied, almost choking on the words.

A plan was quickly made. Leaving the column under the command of Mora's sergeant, along with five of the lancers to ensure that the Mexican guards did not make off with the pack train, Kodosczy led his remaining fifteen lancers in a wide detour off the main road. He took Mora with him, because, as he said, Mora knew where the ambush was to be sprung. But Mora realized that Kodosczy probably did not completely trust him and wanted him where he could keep an eye on him. A good officer, Mora thought. Too bad.

They ambushed the ambushers. Mora led the Hungarians around behind the little canyon where Márquez's men were waiting, about forty of them. A damned bunch of cutthroats, Mora thought, looking down at them from his vantage point on a small hill. He rather suspected that Márquez did not intend that he, Mora, live through the day's work. The fewer tongues that could wag . . .

Kodosczy skillfully moved his men closer. The soldiers below, if one could call them soldiers, were busy watching the trail ahead, those who were not drinking or gambling. Kodosczy drew his men up, softly ordered them to draw their carbines, dressed the line of beautifully accoutered horsemen with his eyes, then brought his sword up. "Fire!" he shouted.

Fifteen carbines roared. At least a dozen of the men below fell, writhing. A sharp order, and the carbines slid back into their saddle scabbards. "Forward . . . at the walk," Kodosczy called out.

Lances raised high, pennants fluttering, the thin line of lancers moved forward. "Trot!" Kodosczy ordered, then a moment later, "At the gallop . . . *charge!*"

The horses leaped forward, the sound of their hooves rising to thunder. Down came the lances, the points glittering in the bright sunlight. The riders were silent, intent. In front of them, pandemonium. Márquez's men had been thrown into disorder by the sudden shattering volley and then the terrible charge. Penned up in their little valley, they could not slip away to the sides.

The lines of lancers smashed into them. Mora, riding to one side, coolly picked off men with the .44 caliber 1860 Army Colt that his father had given him when he rode off to war. He saw a fleeing man run down by a lancer. The lance tip went into the man's back, then reappeared in front of his chest accompanied by a bright spray of blood. With a practiced twist of his arm, the lancer cleared his lance point, flipping the dying man to one side.

More lances went home, until the little battleground became too cramped, and then it was swords and pistols as the attacking cavalry continued to scythe through their opponents, the awful sound of blade against flesh, the lancers hacking down at unprotected heads, thrusting at throats, men screaming. Horses neighed and kicked, tearing at the enemy with their teeth.

It was over in less than a minute, the lancers still in their saddles finishing off those of the enemy who were too badly hurt to run away. A quick count showed one lancer dead and two wounded, but not too badly to ride. Kodosczy looked around at the carnage, then saluted Mora with his bloody sword. "I owe you a considerable debt," Kodosczy said. The words stung Mora.

A short while later the pack train came into view farther down the now-safe trail. A half hour was spent burying the fallen lancer, and then they were on their way again, Kodosczy and the lancers once more riding in front. Mora rode halfway up one side of the pack train, about forty yards behind the lancers. He tried to hide his tension, but it grew and grew, until at last he sighted the place where Valdez would make his move. It was well placed for an ambush, a much better site than the one Márquez's people had chosen. On the left side of the trail a sheer cliff rose up. No escape in that direction. On the other side a number of large boulders came close to the trail. Mora watched as the lancers rode into the trap. Kodosczy seemed to sense something; he looked to his right, inspecting the boulders. Or perhaps it was simply his military sense. This was a good place for an ambush, so why not be cautious? He turned around in his saddle and looked at Mora, but Mora continued to ride easily, as if totally unconcerned. Kodosczy smiled at him and had just turned around to the front again when the first volley burst from the rocks.

Half the lancers went down at once. Kodosczy tried to move the remainder of his men back, but the mules blocked the way. He waved frantically for Mora to move his men around to one side and try to get behind the rocks. Some of the men started to move, but Mora motioned to his sergeant, who was in on the plan, and the sergeant's bellow froze the Mexican troopers into place.

Kodosczy understood then. He shouted something at Mora, the words lost beneath the crash of gunfire, but Mora sensed what the words were, and they made him flinch. Kodosczy raised his pistol and aimed it straight at Mora. Mora refused to move, sat his horse facing the muzzle of that pistol, refusing to defend himself. Kodosczy hesitated for an instant, and then it was too late. A bullet smashed into his neck from the side and he pitched over the side of his horse. Mora continued to sit his mount as Valdez's people burst from their hiding places in the rocks and shattered the last resistance of the Hungarians. Kodosczy rose up on one elbow and shot one of the attackers in the face, then a hail of bullets pounded him over onto his back.

CHAPTER THIRTEEN

It was over even more quickly than the ambush of Márquez's men. Those of Mora's troopers who had not been in on it were told to ride for their lives. None hesitated. One quick look at Valdez's *guerrilleros* and they were pounding back down the road.

Mora looked around for Valdez, but he was nowhere in sight. It was Gutierrez, Valdez's right-hand man, who finally rode up to the lieutenant. "Congratulations," Gutierrez said. "It was perfect."

Mora nodded curtly. He had never liked Gutierrez. He appeared to be more bandit than soldier. He wondered why a patriot like Valdez thought so highly of him. Ah well, in times like these, choosing one's associates with too much care was a luxury long past.

"We had better get moving," Gutierrez said.

"Perhaps it would be best to find a strong place and stay put," Mora suggested. "We could send out a few men to look for one of Porfirio's patrols."

"To find Díaz?" Gutierrez asked in amazement. "For the love of God, why?"

"Why, to give him the gold. The weapons it would buy . . ."

"Ha!" Gutierrez snorted. "This money will not go to Díaz. Not one single gold piece. I have my orders. We march north."

Mora did not know what to say. The gold must be going to the main army, then. To Juárez. Mora knew, everybody knew, that there was considerable tension between Juárez, the great civilian, and Díaz, the great soldier. The war of liberation was coming to an end. How sad to think that after all Mexico's terrible sacrifices of the past several years, its leaders must now settle down to sniping at one another.

However, there was not much that Mora could do. All of his men had run off except his sergeant. More than thirty of Gutierrez's men had survived the fight. Best to go along.

He did think of riding off on his own to look for Díaz, to offer him his services, but he quickly rejected the idea. For one thing, he thought it his duty to keep an eye on the gold. He did not quite trust Gutierrez. And from the way Gutierrez was watching him, he wondered if Gutierrez would simply let him ride away, to carry the tale of the gold to other ears. Perhaps Gutierrez didn't quite trust him, either.

They started north, avoiding settled areas, ducking out of sight whenever military patrols came near. Mora was in agreement with this practice. With anarchy ruling the war-torn nation, half a million pounds sterling in portable wealth was a magnet that would draw untold numbers of desperate men.

Mora began to grow nervous as they headed farther and farther north. They passed Querétaro. One of Gutierrez's men, riding into a village, discovered that the war was basically over. Querétaro had fallen. The Emperor was General Escobedo's prisoner. The former mule driver had triumphed over the Austrian aristocrat. All the action was to the south of them now, and still Gutierrez made no move to seek out Juárez.

Mora asked him. Gutierrez looked coldly at the young lieutenant. Ex-lieutenant now, Mora supposed. "We continue north," Gutierrez said. "The gold goes to Valdez. He is already waiting for us."

In a sense, Mora could not argue too much with that, either. Let Valdez hold the gold until Juárez and the legitimate Mexican government was once again back in the National Palace. There would be great need for money then, to rebuild the shattered economy. Yes, that might be best— the gold in the hands of a trustworthy man.

Mora did trust Valdez. He had met him several times over the past year, in Mexico City. Valdez appeared to move easily in all circles, including the Imperial Court. He had seen through Mora's pretended allegiance with apparent ease. "You are for the Fatherland," Valdez had bluntly said one night at a diplomatic reception, when he and Mora were out of earshot of any others. Mora had been startled, half expecting guards to come running and arrest him. Valdez had quickly put him at his ease. "We are on the same side," he murmured quickly, watching out of the corner of his eye as a fat, drunken Imperial general bore down on them. "I will be in touch with you."

Mora's first reaction was that Valdez was one of Díaz's men, there to relay Díaz's orders and to take Mora's inside information back to Republican headquarters. This did not prove to be the case. Eventually, Díaz's couriers made independent contact with Mora. Then Valdez surfaced again, this time contriving to spend more than an hour alone with Mora. Valdez intimated that he was in a position to do great things for Mexico, and that he would welcome Mora's help. A system was set up in which Mora could get in touch with Valdez at very short notice.

When orders came from General Márquez concerning the English gold, Mora frantically tried to contact his link with Díaz, only to find that the man had recently been discovered and slain while fleeing. In desperation, Mora sent a message to Valdez, who showed up within an hour. Thinking back, Mora remembered how Valdez's eyes had glittered when he told him about the gold. It had been impressive to watch how quickly Valdez organized a plan, the very plan which now had the gold safely away from the Imperialists and heading north. Yes, Valdez was clearly a man to be reckoned with, even if he did keep around him men like Gutierrez.

The road north was not an easy one. Several times vicious little fights were necessary so that they could continue on their route. Bandits swarmed everywhere in a countryside long since severed from all central control. One by one, more than half of Gutierrez's force was killed. Mora's sergeant died too, killed in a savage ambush north of Durango.

Gutierrez had been closemouthed about their final destination. Now he let Mora in on the secret: Chihuahua. Ah yes, Mora thought, the perfect place to conceal anything. Chihuahua, the natural retreat for any man on the outs with the central authority.

The route became more difficult physically, if a little safer militarily. They were now deep into the Sierra Madre mountain range. The country was very dry, and incredibly rugged. Not so much danger now from disaffected troops. The only people they saw for days on end were small groups of Indians, from tribes that, even after centuries of domination, had managed to avoid being Hispanicized. They still lived within their ancient Indian traditions. For the most part, these Indians were content to let the well-armed Mexicans alone. It would continue this way until they got far enough north to have to begin to worry about the dreaded Apaches.

It was a full month after the taking of the gold before they finally reached Valdez. They had already heard that the war was over, Mexico City taken by Díaz, Juárez ready to enter in triumph and resume his presidency, Maximilian locked away in a cell.

Valdez's stronghold turned out to be in a small mountain valley northwest of Cuauhtémoc, near the Sonora border. It was an easily defended place, with the only ingress being through narrow passes. A large stone structure crowned a rocky hill at the upper end of the valley. As the battered little caravan drew closer, Mora could see that the place was actually a fortress, if a rude one. A thick wall enclosed several stone buildings, one of them quite large. They had been passed through by sentries guarding one of the pass entrances, and obviously someone had ridden ahead with the news, because armed men began boiling out of the fortress, riding down toward them. They fanned out around the mule train and its escort, shouting greetings to the survivors. My God, what a rough-looking bunch! Mora thought. *Guerrilleros*, all of them, not a proper uniform among them. They were all dressed in rude frontier clothing, wearing towering sombreros with high peaks and huge upturned brims. Some wore boots, some had only leather-thonged huaraches. All were armed to the teeth, and with the finest weapons, including a few of the new Spencer repeating carbines.

Valdez was waiting in front of the largest structure, which turned out to be both his headquarters and his living space. A salute from Gutierrez, which Valdez returned, but an *abrazo* for Mora, a back-slapping embrace, which Mora could see Gutierrez resented.

"Ah, Lieutenant, I see you have been successful," Valdez said.

"Lieutenant no longer, señor," Mora said ruefully. He had long ago torn off the hated epaulets that marked him as a member of the Imperial forces.

Mora was invited inside to wash and refresh himself. A comfortable room was put at his disposal, complete with a diminutive Indian woman who was to be his maid. Mora was not made uncomfortable by this; it was simply the manner in which he had always lived. To him, the self-effacing little Indian, gliding silently about the room, picking up his discarded and filthy clothing, was practically invisible. He bathed, shaved, dressed in fresh clothing he found laid out on his bed, and then went in to dinner with Valdez.

The dining room was palatial, if a bit drafty. Heavy, ancient wooden furniture gleamed dully in the dim light. Silver candlesticks guttered valiantly against the growing evening gloom. The table setting was of the finest china and silver, and the food surprisingly sumptuous and varied for such a remote location. Valdez knew how to live well, and once again Mora simply accepted it as natural. This was how he himself had always lived.

Valdez, pouring out the brandy after dinner, insisted on hearing all the details of the taking of the gold and of the difficult journey north, although Mora suspected that he had already heard most of the essentials from Gutierrez. It was only at the end of his account that Mora asked the vital question, the question that he owed it to Mexico to ask. "And what is to become of all that money, señor?"

Was there a slight hooding of Valdez's eyes before he replied? The beginnings of evasion? Mora could not tell. Valdez's words were reassuring enough. "It is to be a down payment on the rebuilding of Mexico," he said quietly.

"And when is that to be?"

Valdez looked down at the cigar he held in his hand. "That depends on the politicians in the capital," he finally said. "They . . . may not make it easy. Already there are reports of fighting between them, and the war only just over. If we were to pour that money into the public coffers now, with such anarchy prevailing, well, you know as well as I do, Manuel, that it would disappear forever into the pockets of a bunch of political thieves."

Mora could not argue with that. He was painfully familiar with the history of constant political trauma that had afflicted his country ever since it had gained its independence from Spain less than fifty years before. But still . . .

"And until then?" Mora prompted.

"Why," Valdez said, putting down his cigar and picking up his brandy, "we wait here. What else?"

"We?"

"Of course. After all, what is there to go back to, Manuel?"

Mora did not reply at once. Suddenly he found himself thinking about Valdez differently than he had thought about him before. Valdez was not a big man. He was, in fact, rather smallish, almost unassuming, usually dressed like an intellectual in dark, unobtrusive clothing. Now, listening to him, noticing for the first time the hard, one might almost say ruthless, look in his eyes, and noticing that the clothing was now a little more martial, Mora sensed that he had better keep his mouth shut. "Of course," he agreed. "What is back there . . . after all?"

But he knew better. Back there was action, the government, things were happening, things that would mold the future of Mexico. There was his hero, Porfirio Díaz, and of course his family. For the first time in weeks Mora wondered how his father and sister were weathering the political storms. Mora wanted to be a part of all that action, but he said nothing to Valdez. No, Valdez hardly wanted an idealistic young mouth carrying word of his golden treasure back to the rapacious men in Mexico City.

It was Gutierrez who, about a month later, convinced Mora that he must leave and leave soon. Gutierrez obviously resented Mora's high standing with his *jefe*. The reason for that high standing was, as Valdez himself explained to Mora one night over the inevitable after-dinner brandy, one of intellectual loneliness. "How wonderful to speak to a civilized person again, Manuel. These . . . cattle that I am surrounded with. They are necessary, of course, but . . ."

Mora helped in the hiding of the gold. Only he, Valdez, and Gutierrez were involved, taking the four gold-laden mules up to the head of the valley one afternoon while the bulk of the little garrison was conveniently out of the way on a rather unnecessary scouting mission. Gutierrez led the way to a cave hidden in a cul-de-sac at the end of a rugged little arroyo. The cave mouth was a mere slit half obscured by brush, but the cave inside was large and dry. It took the three of them the whole afternoon to move the gold inside. Later, as they once again pulled brush over the cave opening, Mora, turning around, caught Gutierrez looking at him in a most malevolent and unsettling manner, and it was then that Mora suspected he would probably soon meet with an unfortunate "accident."

He left a week later, slipping away in the night up a narrow path he had discovered near the head of the valley. He had told Valdez that he was going hunting, and since there appeared to be no way out of the valley other than past these sentries, he had a considerable start before his absence was discovered. He left a note behind, explaining to Valdez his motives for returning to Mexico City and becoming involved in the coming political struggles. In the same note he promised Valdez that word of the gold would never leave his lips.

If there was pursuit, it was unsuccessful. The journey to the south in itself came close to being fatal. The nearer Mora got to the center of the country, the more the countryside teemed with ragged bands of men who would be happy to kill him for his horse, saddle, and weapons.

He arrived in the city tired, hungry, and dirty, and immediately headed for the family home. It was a large establishment built around a central inner courtyard, in the old Spanish style. It looked unusually dark and forbidding to Mora as he rode up to it. All of the shutters of the upper windows were closed. The huge front doors leading into the courtyard and stables were firmly shut too.

He had banged on the doors for some time before he heard footsteps approaching from inside. Slowly a small door set into the bigger doors opened. Mora found himself facing a little man who was obviously a servant but looked like a bandit. "What do you want?" he asked Mora in a surly voice.

"I am looking for Señor Mora," Manuel said. He had never seen this man before. Had his father been reduced to hiring riffraff such as this for servants?

The man snarled and spat on the ground, not too far from Mora's boots. "Old Tomaso Mora?" he sneered. "That Emperor-loving traitor? He was sent packing a long time ago."

"What? But this is his house!"

"Not any longer. It belongs to Arístides Gomez now. And just who the hell are you, anyhow?"

Mora seized the man by the throat and dragged him near, at the same time drawing his Colt and pressing the muzzle against the base of the man's nose. "I'll tell you who I am, maggot," he said quietly. "My name is Manuel Mora, the son of that 'traitor,' Tomaso Mora. Now, tell me where I can find him, or..."

The man, staring cross-eyed at the muzzle of Mora's pistol, babbled his innocence of any information relating to Mora's father or sister. Mora shoved him back into the courtyard and stalked away. It took him the rest of the day, looking up friends of the family, most of whom were very hard to find, to discover that his father and sister had fled the city and were now living on the family's country estate. Well, they should be safe there, Mora thought in relief. He considered riding to join them, but it was a considerable journey, and he wanted to put off meeting his father as long as possible. For the time being, there were things to do, people to see.

Working out of an inn, Mora over the next few days collected a picture of what had been happening in the city since he had left it more than three months before. The Emperor had been executed in June. Mora knew that. Díaz had taken the city shortly before. What he had not known was the intensity of the struggle between the architects of the fight against the French. Mora gathered information avidly. He was told by an admirer that Díaz had turned over his entire army—with which he could easily have seized the supreme power—along with a considerable treasury, to Juárez.

"Like a modern Cincinnatus," the admirer said.

"Like the conniving devil he is," a detractor replied.

Juárez had finally entered the city in July—and coolly snubbed his premier military commander, insulting one of the few men who might have helped him right the chaos Mexico had become. The treasury was bankrupt. Mobs of ex-soldiers, thoughtlessly dismissed from active service by Juárez, who distrusted the military from the very center of his soul, wandered the countryside, starving, looting, killing. New revolts were springing up among the very men who had fought for national independence. While himself remaining loyal to the government.' Díaz had refused to fight against his former comrades in arms. The entire country was once again tearing at its own throat.

Mora finally went to see Díaz, wondering if the man would remember him. Surely, one so important . . . But Díaz was overjoyed to see the ex-lieutenant. "But I thought you must be dead!" he exclaimed.

Díaz was in full general's uniform, with its heavily brocaded crossed lapels, gold-encrusted epaulets, high collar, gold buttons; a tall, broad-shouldered man with heavy mustaches and a Vandyke beard. Somewhat hooded Indian eyes, high cheekbones, and thick straight black hair proclaimed his native blood: Díaz was more Mixtec Indian than Spanish.

He looked every inch the national hero, if somewhat harassed at the moment.

True to his word to Valdez, Mora said nothing about the gold. He merely said that the fighting had taken him far from the city and he had only just now returned. With the quick judgment that was his trademark, Díaz soon realized he had a potential supporter, and he needed supporters. Before long, Mora found himself working for Díaz's candidacy in the upcoming presidential election. It was a bitter campaign, with the specter of armed force always in the background.

Díaz lost the election to Juárez, and embittered, decided to return to his home state of Oaxaca, to the plantation that a grateful Oaxacan government had given him. Mora stayed in the city for a short time, becoming more and more depressed. Finally, after the particularly bloody repression of an attempted revolt by starving citizens, Mora made up his mind. His hero was in eclipse, the government stank to high heaven. He would leave the city and return to the family estate.

CHAPTER FOURTEEN

It was a four-day ride to the Mora hacienda. If anything, the situation in the countryside had deteriorated. Only the fact that Mora was obviously well armed and capable of defending himself permitted him to get through unscathed. On the fourth day he came in sight of the hacienda. It was quite a large place, a jumble of stone and adobe buildings butted up against a steep hill. The surrounding terrain was semitropical; the hacienda was at a much lower elevation than the more than eight thousand feet of Mexico City.

Mora could see people working around the hacienda, tending crops and animals, but the main gates were shut. His arrival seemed to cause a certain amount of consternation. Two men with rifles appeared on top of the adobe wall encircling the main buildings. The heavy front gates remained tightly shut. Mora reined up in front of the gate, and it was only then that a white-haired figure appeared on the wall next to the two riflemen. He stared down at Mora for several seconds, unspeaking.

"Well, Father," Manuel said. "Aren't you going to open the gate?"

Mora's homecoming developed into a scene straight from The Return of the Prodigal Son. Manuel had previously sent word that he was alive, but that had been months ago. His horse and gear were taken from him, and he was led into the main house, a massive colonial masterpiece, and there he saw a lovely young woman he did not at first recognize. His sister! Carmen! "But . . ." he burst out. Carmen had . . . changed. She was now fifteen years old.

The months had changed Mora's father, too; he had aged considerably, was more stooped and worn-looking, but he still exhibited that sense of fierce aliveness that had always awed his son.

There were no recriminations over Manuel's long absence. Carmen clearly adored her older brother; she hung

126

on his every word at dinner. Old Tomaso grumbled a little when Manuel bluntly informed him that he was a partisan of Porfirio Díaz. "Well, the best of that scurvy bunch," the old man finally said.

Later, he told Manuel of the difficulties of living in the country. "It's a constant state of siege. Bandits everywhere. We have to guard ourselves night and day."

Manuel easily fell into the rhythm of life as a *hacendado*, a wealthy Mexican landowner. His father continued to manage the daily operation of the estate, while Manuel oversaw the military side. He soon had a small band of vaqueros whipped into shape as a fairly efficient fighting force. He had been home only three months when he first put them to work. One morning there was smoke on the horizon from the direction of a neighboring *finca*, and an hour later a badly shot-up man came riding in and gasped out the story of an attack by a band of about a dozen men. Before he passed out, he told the Moras that the bandits were heading their way.

Manuel formed up his little group of eight armed and mounted men and was galloping out of the front gate within fifteen minutes. Part of his preparations had been to survey every inch of the surrounding area to look for natural places of ambush or defense. Reaching one of these places, he quickly dispersed his men into prearranged cover, as they had practiced a number of times before. A half hour later a dozen heavily armed and rather drunken horsemen came into view, leading a small string of pack animals. Spoils from the morning's raid, Manuel guessed.

The ensuing action was very short. The dozen raiders, not expecting armed resistance way out here, rode straight into the ambush. At the first volley, those who survived raced their horses toward a brushy area—which contained four of Mora's men. Another withering blast of fire, and the *banditos* wheeled their horses, looking for another way out. But there was none, and they were cut to pieces in the crossfire. Any still alive after the firing stopped were disposed of with a bullet in the head.

Months passed, then a year. Manuel was discovering that he genuinely liked this country life, although sometimes memories of being at the center of the national drama made him restless. The most unsatisfied member of the household was Carmen. All she could talk about was the city. Again and again she coaxed Manuel into recounting to her his impressions of the glittering Imperial Court, and once in a while to describe what he had seen of social life under the restored Republican regime.

It was treachery from within that finally brought down the Mora household. One of the servants, angry over a rebuke, let a band of raiders in through a back entrance very early one morning—and was promptly knifed by the bandits as a reward. The raiders, fifteen of them, had infiltrated deeply into the inner courtyard before they were discovered.

It was not the easy pickings the interlopers had expected. Their intended victims fought back fiercely, but the bandits had the element of surprise on their side, and within a short time several of them were inside the main house. Fighting still raged outside. The Moras, father and son, half dressed, were both firing out into the courtyard from upper floor windows.

But the raiders were behind them now, inside the house. It was Carmen's shrill scream that alerted both men. "Her bedroom!" Manuel shouted, and raced down the hallway ahead of his father.

The door to the girl's bedroom had been kicked off its hinges. Manuel stepped inside. If the raiders had not been so interested in Carmen, Manuel might have been gunned down instantly. There were six men inside her room. The leader of the raiders had backed the girl into a corner and was ripping off her nightgown, laughing hoarsely. The girl fought back grimly. Naked flesh gleamed.

The sight of his sister's half-naked body enraged Manuel. Shouting curses, he shot the bandit closest to him; he could not shoot the man attacking his sister without danger of hitting her. To his right his father's pistol roared and another man fell. The bandit leader, letting go of Carmen, whirled around, his eyes startled, his hand going for his gun. Manuel had just shot another man when the bandit leader's pistol came up. He would have shot Manuel, but Carmen, a true daughter of Mexico, sprang at the man from behind, clawing and biting, ruining his aim.

Gunfire crashed throughout the room as both the bandits and the Moras fought for their lives. Old Tomaso shot another man, then took a bullet in the chest. Manuel knew that his father was hit, saw him going down, but he had no time to spare. The bandit leader had shoved Carmen away and shot at Manuel, missing. Manuel, shooting back too quickly, hit the man in the shoulder, spinning him around, knocking the gun from the bandit's hand.

There was only one bandit left on his feet now, and he tried to fire at Manuel, but his pistol was empty. Cursing, he reached for the machete he wore at his side, trying to get to Manuel before Manuel shot him. But Manuel's pistol was empty too. The bandit swung the machete. Manuel ducked under the flat steel blade, stumbling as he wrenched a machete from the dead hand of another of the bandits. Turning, he faced his opponent, raising his machete barely in time to ward off a downward blow.

Steel clanged against steel. The *bandito* dodged back as Manuel lunged at him and missed. Both men edged cautiously toward one another, panting. Meanwhile, Carmen, kicking off the ruins of her nightgown, was scrambling around on the floor, looking for the wounded bandit leader's pistol.

The bandit with the machete lunged again. Manuel faded back, letting him overextend, then his own machete whipped out and down, hacking into the man's arm above the elbow. Blood spurted. The man staggered back, his eyes wide with pain. Manuel charged after him, raised his machete high, then buried it in the man's skull.

Then an oath behind him, and Manuel, spinning around, saw another bandit standing in the doorway, leveling a pistol at him. Manuel drew his arm back, intending to throw the machete, knowing that he did not have enough time; the bandit's bullet would reach him first. Then a roar from behind Manuel and the bandit reeled backward, a bright stain of blood quickly blossoming in the center of his white blouse.

Turning, Manuel saw his sister, totally naked, with a smoking pistol in her hand. He saw her turn then to face the wounded bandit leader, who was trying to crawl toward a pistol lying a few feet away. Carmen ran toward him and straddled his body. He looked upward, up those long lovely naked legs, past the wispy triangle at her thighs, past the breasts he had so brutally fondled, into Carmen's hate-filled eyes.

"You son of a whore," she said softly, and blew the top of his head off.

There was no more shooting outside. The last of the bandits had been killed—along with most of the defenders, including their patriarch, Don Tomaso Mora, who lay dead in his daughter's bedroom. However, the bandits in their rage, when they knew they were losing, had fired the house. Smoke was already pouring into the upper floors.

The fires were eventually brought under control, but most of the building was in ruins. Manuel, after burying his father, thought of rebuilding, but it was Carmen, once again wearing clothes—he would never forget that image of her, naked, the smoking pistol in her hand—talked him out of it. "Let's leave this place," she said vehemently. "If we aren't killed by bandits, we'll die of boredom. At least *I* will."

Mora wavered, but eventually his mind was made up when a letter arrived—from Díaz. It seemed that the general's political hopes were reviving. He asked Manuel if he would go to the capital and make contact with some of his supporters there. Once again energized by the prospect of becoming involved in his country's political evolution, Mora informed Carmen that they would be leaving at once for the city.

He had never before seen a woman pack so quickly.

CHAPTER FIFTEEN

The Mora survivors trekked to the capital in a small convoy, taking with them the last of the cattle and sheep, which were to be sold in the city for the money they would need to live on. After years of civil war, there was little left of the Mora fortune except those animals and the burned-out hacienda.

In the city, Mora rented a large house and staffed it with his former country retainers. He saw to it that Carmen was able to buy the latest dresses and be seen in the best social circles. The financial drain was heavy, however, and he knew they would not be able to maintain that kind of lifestyle for very long.

Porfirio Díaz was in the capital, once again in politics as a national deputy in the Congress. His popularity was growing day by day, but still he refused to have anything to do with any overt plots against Juárez's government. He preferred to wait for the elections.

He spent a great deal of time with Mora, and bit by bit the younger man began to understand the extent of the other's ambition. It was all or nothing. Ah well, Mora said to himself. So he is not as unselfish as we once thought. But then, who is?

However, on one trip to Oaxaca to visit Díaz after he had resigned his seat in Congress and returned to his *finca*, Mora was further surprised to find that Felix Díaz, Porfirio's younger brother, was raising a strong military force. Mora was uneasy around Felix. There was a wildness and cruelty about the man that he did not trust.

Then the elections. Díaz polled nearly the same number of votes as Juárez. The final decision fell on Congress. Juárez was chosen, with his old vice-president, Sebastián Lerdo, still second in line. The Porfiristas were enraged, crying, "Fraud!" There was talk of armed revolt, but Díaz, sensing that the time was not quite ripe, tried to calm his

131

partisans. No use. Armed revolt broke out in the city. A drunken government general, Sostenes Rocha, entered the capital with loyal troops, and a wholesale slaughter began.

Mora was forced out of the city with Díaz; he was too closely allied with him in the public mind to escape danger. He left Carmen behind in their big house, trusting that her sex would save her from danger.

Once back in Oaxaca, Díaz proclaimed a call to arms against the government. To his surprise the province responded poorly. His small forces were quickly crushed. He fled with a few followers, including his brother and Mora, toward the center of the country, certain that the citizens of Mexico City would rise for him. They did not. Díaz had no choice but to abandon his small cavalry escort and flee.

"Well, my friend," he said to Mora, "it looks as if this comedy is played out."

Mora insisted on staying with Díaz. There was still hope; three other rebel generals remained in the field. Then, like a thunderbolt, Sostenes Rocha, with bottles of brandy in his holsters instead of pistols, swept down on them and smashed their armies. The revolt was over.

The news became worse. Felix Díaz, while sacking a village and murdering the locals, was overwhelmed by a superior force. The enraged inhabitants flayed the skin from the soles of his feet and forced him to march through the streets, tracking blood, while they slowly beat and stoned him to death.

Mora was desolate as he fled with his revered leader. He now began to see changes in the man, or rather, to be more clearly aware of signs that he had noticed before but had not cared to acknowledge. Díaz, bitter and frightened, but still lusting for power, was now ready to accept help from wherever he could get it. He quite easily jettisoned his earlier liberal principles and began to treat with his former conservative enemies.

The nadir was when Díaz, disguised as a priest, with Mora at his side, made his way secretly to the mountain lair of Manuel Lozada, *cacique* of the Nayarit Indians. Lozada was famous for his brutality and superstition, espousing a weird blend of Catholicism and ancient Indian religious rituals. He made no secret that his aim was to lead a war against the white man and establish a "holy" Indian empire, an empire that a man like Díaz, despite his Indian blood, could have no part in.

Díaz went to Lozada hat in hand, smiling ingratiatingly as he asked for asylum from the government, whose troops did not dare enter Lozada's mountain domain. Mora was there to watch it, to see his idol step forward to give Lazada the *abrazo*, but Lozada coolly held him off, offering instead a frigid handshake, He did, however, grant Díaz a place to temporarily hide out from the government.

A number of Díaz's supporters remained with him in Nayarit, but not Mora. His ideals had exploded in his face. He suddenly saw no future for himself in Mexico—an outlaw, without funds, no personal following to fall back on, disillusioned. For the first time in years he began to think again of Valdez . . . and of five hundred thousand pounds sterling in golden British sovereigns.

Slipping out of Lozada's stronghold, he made his way to the city, traveling by night. No one paid any attention to the ragged traveler who rode through the capital's streets early one morning and knocked at the door of a large house. Mora slipped inside the moment the servant opened it. "Call Señorita Carmen," he ordered.

She came out, blinking, a dressing gown over her nightgown, and Mora was reminded of that day two years before, when she had fought, naked, alongside himself and their father. She was nineteen now, almost twenty, and her earlier girlish loveliness had matured into a radiant beauty. "Manuel!" she burst out on seeing him. "I thought you were—"

"Dead again?" Mora replied bitterly. "Never quite all the way dead. At least not physically. But I am certainly dead politically, economically, and socially. And so are you, Carmen."

Carmen nodded. It was no secret to her that the family

fortune was completely depleted. Creditors had been hounding her for weeks. She had even begun selling her ball gowns. "What can we do?" she asked.

Mora gave her a bare outline of his plans, although he did not directly mention Valdez or the gold, only that he had a way of raising a considerable amount of money. "But we will have to go to the United States," he informed her. "It would be too dangerous to remain in Mexico."

Carmen was all for it. "Wonderful!" she exclaimed. "New Orleans. New York. Perhaps we could even go to Europe."

Carmen was told to use the last of her money to purchase a steamship ticket to New Orleans. Mora would wire her when it was time to leave. He himself left at dawn the next morning, slipping quietly out of the city and pointing his horse north, toward Chihuahua.

Riding alone, he made the trip quickly. The closer he got to Valdez's little valley, the more tense he grew. He knew that he was about to perform one of the most dangerous acts in an already adventurous life.

He stayed for the night in a small inn about ten miles from the valley. What he did not know was that one of Valdez's men was standing at the bar of the inn as Mora went upstairs with his saddlebags. The man recognized him, and after downing one more hasty drink, rode straight for the valley.

In the morning, Mora made his final plans. There was always the option of riding straight up to one of the guarded passes that led into the valley and asking to be taken to Valdez. The man had liked him well enough once. Perhaps he would . . .

But no. It would be idiocy to put himself in Valdez's hands, to trust in the man's good nature. There had been that look in his eyes. Better to do it the way he had planned.

Mora bought a packhorse and pack saddle from the innkeeper, then rode off into the mountains, making a big circle around Valdez's valley. It was the next morning before he finally found the faint game track that led up into the hills toward the little trail he had ridden out on five years before.

It was harder going this time, leading the packhorse, but not impossible. As he rode, Mora wondered if the money was still where he had helped hide it. Five years was a long time. Perhaps Valdez had either used or rehidden the gold. But he had not heard of any infusions of cash of that magnitude into Mexico's turbulent politics. No, the money must still be there.

He came out near the cave in the early afternoon. For over an hour he sat on his horse, listening. Nothing. Cautiously he rode closer. Yes, there was the entrance, still screened by brush. With his heart beating quickly, he cleared away the entrance and, lighting a torch, stepped inside. Yes, there it was, stacked neatly. The gold.

He went outside again to bring in the pack saddle. Working quickly, he stuffed it full of all the gold it would safely hold, roughly two hundred pounds' weight of gold coin, in value about ten thousand pounds sterling, or fifty thousand dollars American. A fortune, but still only a small percentage of the entire five hundred thousand pounds, and certainly his due. If it were not for him . . . For a moment he had a very vivid image of Captain Count Kodosczy and his glittering lancers.

He staggered outside with the heavily laden pack saddle. It was all he could do to hoist it up onto the horse's back. A growing feeling of tension spurred him on. There was something wrong here—he could sense it. What it was he discovered a moment later, when, hearing gravel crunch behind him, he spun around and found himself facing Gutierrez, who had just emerged from behind some brush and was now pointing a pistol straight at Mora's belly.

"You!" Mora burst out.

Gutierrez favored him with a cold smile. "Yes, me. Surprised?"

Mora slumped dejectedly. "Not really."

"We got word yesterday night that you were in the vicinity," Gutierrez said. "Valdez is with the others, at the main pass, waiting for you. I knew that was a mistake. I always suspected you left by some other route and would probably come back the same way. And there was no doubt in my mind as to where you would be heading. To steal the gold!"

"Steal?" Mora burst out. "It was I who took it in the first place—along with you. Not Valdez. If anyone has a right to some of this gold, it's you and me."

Gutierrez chuckled. "And how far do you think either of us would get? Valdez has a passion for loyalty. Cheat him, or even let him think you cheated him, and he'll spend the rest of his days tracking you down."

"A chance I'm willing to take. And what does it matter? There's always someone in this country tracking you down."

"Ah, but you see, I have a passion for loyalty too. And now Valdez will see that I do. His judgment was blinded before—by you!" Gutierrez's voice was becoming a little shrill. "Now I'll show him for certain just who it is he can count on. And when he has the supreme power, this pile of gold will seem like a beggar's pocketful to those of us who stay with him all the way."

Only at the end of his little speech did Gutierrez become aware of the slow widening of Mora's eyes. Mora was staring past Gutierrez. For a moment Gutierrez thought Mora was trying to trick him. He took a small step to the side, keeping his eyes on Mora, and as he moved, his right leg nearly brushed the big rattlesnake coiled on a rock next to him.

It was the warning buzz of the rattles that finally alerted Gutierrez. He spun, aiming his pistol at the snake, but a second too late. The snake struck, sinking its fangs into his leg. Gutierrez screamed and backed away. The snake reared, ready to strike again. Gutierrez's shot tore the snake's head off, but by then Mora was on him, wrestling the pistol from his grasp.

Gutierrez sat down heavily, his hands clutching his thigh just above where the snake had struck. He looked up at Mora, a mixture of hatred and fear in his eyes. He fully expected Mora to shoot him; that's what he would have done if the circumstances had been reversed. Mora considered it, but despite all the killing he had been involved in over the past few years, the idea didn't appeal to him. The snake venom would probably finish Gutierrez anyhow. "Do you have a horse here?" he asked Gutierrez.

"Behind those rocks," Gutierrez said dully, staring down at the two fang holes in his pants leg.

Mora ran up the little arroyo and returned a minute later leading Gutierrez's mount. "You'll understand that I cannot wait here to help you," he said to Gutierrez. "Put a tourniquet on the bite, and ride like hell for Valdez and the others."

He did not expect any gratitude from Gutierrez, nor did he get it. The man glared after him as he rode away leading the packhorse. He did his best to cover his tracks as he followed his secret route out of the valley, but he had to move fast. Gutierrez's shot might have alerted Valdez and his men.

He made it out of the valley without incident and rode for the next twenty-four hours straight, stopping only to rest the horses a few minutes. He used every trick he knew to cover his tracks. The terrain helped. For long distances he was able to ride over huge stretches of barren rock, changing direction frequently before coming out again onto ground that would show his tracks.

On the third day he reached a town with a telegraph and wired Carmen to leave Mexico City. A week more of hard riding before he finally crossed into the United States, unnoticed by anyone along that desolate stretch of border that separated Mexico and West Texas. A brief rest, and then, by stage and train, he worked his way east, arriving in New Orleans a week after Carmen.

He found her in the hotel he had told her to use. She was delighted to see him, and even more delighted to discover that they once again had money. She loved New Orleans and enthusiastically entered its social life. Too enthusiastically. Word got around, and one day Mora was startled to see one of Valdez's men watching him from a street corner. There was no choice but to flee, to New York this time, which Carmen loved even more than New Orleans.

He was able to follow news of Mexico in the newspapers, and by talking to other refugees. In July, a thunderbolt. Benito Juárez, President of Mexico and national hero, died in office. His vice-president, Sebastián Lerdo, was president now, and offering amnesty to those who had revolted against Juárez. How bitter a pill for Díaz! Juárez had once offered him the vice-presidency. If only he had accepted, he would be president now. Enraged by the blows of fate, Díaz at first spurned amnesty and tried to maintain his revolt, but Lerdo was too popular with the Mexican people.

The noose tightened. Díaz's implacable enemy, Sostenes Rocha, was hot on his trail, anxious to finish off Díaz before Lerdo spoiled his fun with his damned amnesty plan. With nowhere to turn, Díaz finally accepted amnesty and retired, sullenly, to a sugar plantation near Veracruz, and as far as Mora was able to ascertain, was presently living a simple and industrious life.

Mora too thought about accepting amnesty and returning to Mexico, but . . . in Mexico there would always be the problem of Valdez.

Sensing that another move was imminent, Carmen suggested that they go to Europe, but Mora was beginning to yearn for people of his own culture, for his own language. By now he was suffering the unique torments of the exile, remembering the sights, the tastes, the smells of his native land. He was also remembering how pleasant he had found life on the Mora estate. Yes, that might be the answer—a ranch somewhere in the United States, perhaps one of those states that had a Mexican community. He quickly ruled out Texas and New Mexico—they were too close to Chihuahua and Sonora . . . and to Valdez. So then it must be California!

Thus it was that Mora and his sister, Carmen, complaining bitterly as the train took them west deeper and deeper into horrifyingly primitive country, made their way to the backwater of rural San Diego County, as isolated a place as Mora could find and still live within his Latin culture.

After years of being involved in other people's quests for power, Mora now chose for himself . . . obscurity.

CHAPTER SIXTEEN

Yet the world of action had followed Mora into his obscurity, and now he lay dying, a bullet from his past lodged inside his chest.

By the time Mora had finished the last of his story, the wagon Diego had sent for had arrived. They gently lifted him into it, his head on Carmen's lap, his blood staining her dress. The wagon moved off slowly, Mora's men, along with Doc and Raider, riding alongside. It took them more than an hour to reach the hacienda. Each mile Mora grew visibly weaker.

"He's not going to make it," Doc murmured to Raider.

When they had reached a little rise that overlooked the hacienda, Mora murmured something to his sister. Carmen signaled for the wagon to stop. "He wants to look at it from here," she said.

The wagon stopped. Mora managed to struggle to a half-sitting position, Carmen partially supporting him. For several minutes he looked at his land, his house, his animals; then he lay back and died.

Carmen began to cry. The vaqueros swore quietly. The wagon started up again and took Mora to the house, where his body was lifted out and taken inside. Doc saw that Carmen was now dry-eyed. He did not like the look on her face.

Raider pulled him aside. "What the hell we gonna do?" he asked in a low voice.

"I don't know," Doc replied. "We're not in a good position. If Mora was telling the truth, and he had no reason to lie when he was dying, then the gold isn't here at all, only what he took from Valdez, and I suspect that most of it went into this place. All we know is that it's somewhere in northern Chihuahua; he never got around to telling us just where Valdez's place is."

"Somewhere near Cua . . . something like that."

140

"Cuauhtémoc. We could look it up on a map."

"And never find that valley. Uh-uh, Doc, I think we gotta follow Gutierrez . . . and Logan. I wonder what the hell his part is in this?"

Doc had no answer for that. But he did agree that the best move was to follow Gutierrez. With luck he'd lead them to Valdez. The time to leave was now. No point in letting their quarry get too big a start. And then, there was Carmen. He remembered the look of contempt on her face when she'd found out he was a Pinkerton. That was a look he didn't want to face again, not now at least. Maybe later— when she got over the death of her brother.

Doc went to see Diego and asked to buy a horse. Diego instantly offered to give him one. "You are going after those *hijos de putas,*" he said savagely. "I know it. Wait a day until we bury Don Manuel, and I and half the vaqueros will ride with you."

It was a tempting offer, to have a strong force with them; following Gutierrez to Valdez was going to be like following a tiger into its lair. But on the other hand, what about the gold? No, the fewer people involved in this, the better. Doc told Diego that they could not wait a day, that they must leave at once or the trail would grow cold. Diego reluctantly agreed, but he still insisted on giving Doc a horse. He also promised to take care of Judith and the wagon until Doc returned. An hour later, without Doc seeing Carmen again, he and Raider were riding out of the ranch yard, mounted, armed, and with supplies for several days.

They rode straight to the little depression where Mora had been shot. The trail was clear. They set off east, after the broad track of Gutierrez and his men. "I wish we could let the office know where the hell we are and where we're heading," Doc said worriedly, thinking about the telegraphic sending equipment secreted under the floorboards of his wagon. But there were no telegraph wires near anyhow. There was no choice but to ride off into the unknown and take the first opportunity they had to report in.

The trail took them up a broad valley that slowly narrowed, climbing all the while. The countryside was quite beautiful. Although there were very high mountains to their left, and the ground to their right was very rough, they passed through a gentle upland valley of rolling hills and rich pastures. They eventually turned south, camping that night under a large live oak. It was cold.

The next day they passed through the small settlement of Santa Ysabel. Questioning the locals, they were told that a large band of Mexicans had passed through the day before, and not long after, a small force of gringos.

"Logan's following them all the way, then," Doc said.

"Yeah, I seen his sign," Raider murmured. "He wants him as bad as we do."

The trail led farther south, through increasingly rough and dry country. On the third day they crossed the border into Mexico at the tiny Mexican village of Tecate.

"Didn't waste no time in gettin' back on home ground," Raider muttered.

They pushed on, into the dry rocky backcountry of Baja California. It was when they were topping a barren hill that Raider looked back and saw a small moving dot several miles back. "We're bein' followed," he told Doc. "Kinda thought so yesterday, but now I know for sure."

"Do you think any of them could have gotten around behind us?" Doc asked.

"Don't know. But I'm gonna find out."

Raider set up an ambush at a place where the path narrowed to a single track winding between huge boulders. He placed Doc behind one big rock, himself behind another, settling himself in with his rifle cocked and ready. After half an hour both he and Doc could hear the regular hoofbeats of a horse clip-clopping up the stony path. Raider hugged the back of the boulder, letting the lone rider pass by, then he stepped out behind him and leveled his rifle. "Make a move an' your ass belongs to Saint Peter," he said.

The horseman stopped and held perfectly still, looking straight ahead. Doc was posted a little to the front in case the rider made a break for it, and it was he who suddenly realized who it was. "Carmen!" he burst out.

The girl turned at the sound of his voice. "You have been very hard too catch up with," she said. She sounded tired and a little frightened, and her horse was slightly lame.

"Oh, Jesus God," Raider moaned. "This is all we need."

The three of them rode to a small spring a couple of miles farther along, saying nothing until they had dismounted and watered the horses. Carmen's story was simple. She wanted to find the men who had killed her brother.

"An' just what the hell are you gonna do then?" Raider demanded.

She seemed surprised that he needed to ask. "Why, kill them, of course."

"Yeah. Yeah, sure," Raider muttered.

Doc demanded that she go back. She refused. Doc suggested taking her horse and dropping her off at the nearest sign of habitation.

"You'd leave me out here, without a mount, at the mercy of strangers?" she demanded, her voice dripping scorn.

Doc knew it wouldn't work. There was no way to leave her, horse or no horse. If she was mounted, he had no doubt she'd simply continue to follow them. Horseless, she could be in real trouble. Raider explained that the people inhabiting this arid, poverty-stricken area were not known for their gentleness. And there was another factor, too. Her very presence was already lightening the gloom inside Doc's soul. After the few days' separation, the reality of her beauty and aliveness hit him like a hammer blow.

It was finally agreed that she accompany them until they could find a safe place to leave her, although Doc, knowing the girl better than Raider did, doubted she would be that easy to get rid of. He was disturbed by the obvious intensity of her desire to gain revenge over her brother's killers.

They rode on, past Mexicali, paralleling the international border for the most part, until at last they turned southeast at the Sonora border. The country was incredibly wild, and very sparsely settled. And the weather was growing steadily colder. Raider was grateful for the lack of rain so far; the trail they were following was still clear. But let enough rain come and the traces of their quarry would be washed away.

At first, Carmen was cool to Doc; then, little by little, they began to talk. She bitterly accused him of being a spy, of using her to gain family information. He countered by reminding her that he had never asked her anything about her family or her brother. Their relationship had been personal, he insisted, reminding her that *she* had been the one to make the first move.

She softened a little after that and was friendlier. To Doc, that was almost worse than when she had been icy. She was so near physically, but so totally out of his reach. He was, day and night, intensely aware of her desirability. He had never before met so desirable a woman. Despite her obvious breeding, she exuded an animal sensuousness that she seemed to be unaware of. And he had had physical experience of that sensuality. It was torture to have her so close.

Signs began to appear that it was growing difficult for her too. From time to time he caught her sending speculative glances his way. Raider was aware of it too, and he was disgusted. It was bad enough having the girl along, but Doc was acting like a fourteen-year-old boy in love for the first time. Hell, as far as he himself was concerned, give him a woman like Conchita anytime.

Matters took their inevitable course. They had now come to the outlying foothills of the Sierra Nevada. One afternoon they made camp early in a little canyon with a fast-running stream. Carmen walked away from the camp, saying she was going to bathe in the stream. Doc caught the quick nervous glance she threw his way as she walked into the trees. He knew that look. He remained behind at their small campfire for a few minutes, pretending to cook a strip of meat over the coals. He looked up and saw Raider looking back at him. "Go to hell," Doc snarled and, flinging down the meat, walked rapidly away in the direction Carmen had taken.

He could hear her before he saw her; there was the sound of water splashing, of the girl humming some little tune.

He saw her then. She was in the water up to her knees, in a little eddying pool near the bank, away from the faster part of the current. She was naked, bending, splashing water over herself. He could hear her gasp at the coolness of the water.

He stood next to a tree, watching, feeling his body responding. She looked up, saw him, looked away with a sullen defiance that sent a wave of perverse invitation his way. He was moving then, walking toward her. There was no way he could stop himself.

She turned, met him at the water's edge, pressed her body against his. Their lips met. His hands roamed feverishly over her flesh. It was an explosion, his fingers moving between her thighs, her hips bucking mindlessly, hungrily, and then his trousers were down around his ankles and he was sitting on a rock, the girl straddling him, sitting in his lap, grinding her hips down frantically as he stabbed up into her.

It did not last more than a minute or two, but it was nevertheless one of the most intense sexual experiences Doc had ever had. Carmen shuddered above him as he came, and he knew she was coming too. She collapsed in his lap and kissed him. They uncoupled slowly, not saying anything, but he could see from the softness of Carmen's expression that it had been very good for her. But then, it always seemed to be very good for her.

She said nothing to him after they had returned to the campfire. Raider leered a little but had the sense to keep his mouth shut. It was not until twenty-four hours later that Carmen slipped into Doc's bedroll in the middle of the night. They made love more slowly this time, and, after it was over, Carmen held him tightly. "You'll help me, won't you?" she whispered fiercely.

"Help you what?"

"Kill them! Gutierrez. Valdez. The men who killed my brother!"

Doc made no reply, just held her until he knew she was asleep. His mind was in a turmoil. He wanted this girl more than he had ever wanted anything in his life. He tried to plan, to work it out. He sensed he was spinning fantasies, but he could not help himself. Carmen, even if she wanted to stay with him when this was all over, would be a problem— she was in love with a lifestyle he would have trouble supporting.

There was one hope, though. The gold. There was a reward for its return. Pinkerton agents were not eligible for rewards, but perhaps he could leave the agency, claim the reward, which would be one hell of a lot of money, and take Carmen to Europe. Apparently Europe was one of her dreams. Yes, if he had the money . . .

Don't be a fool, he warned himself. It's all smoke. All a pipe dream. Use your head, Doc. Just accept what fate has given you for the time being. Don't try to hold on to her; it would be like holding on to fire. You'd get burned. But my *God* she was worth the risk!

The next day saw them riding up into the high mountains, near the Chihuahua border. The higher they climbed, the colder it got. As the day drew to a close, heavy storm clouds were forming ahead of them.

"I kinda think we oughta find some shelter," Raider said.

They pushed on, and Doc could see that Raider was growing increasingly nervous. "What's the matter?" Doc finally asked.

Raider pointed down to the sign they had been following. "Too damned fresh," he muttered. "We're closin' in on 'em faster than we should. We better make camp now. I sure as hell don't want to come up on 'em in the dark. An' the way those clouds are movin' in . . ."

They made camp inside a shallow cave, more of a rock overhang, really, the three of them sleeping side by side as the thunder crashed, the wind howled, and the rain beat down outside. Doc was grateful for the shelter but upset that it was such a tight fit. With Raider sleeping so close, he felt disinclined to make love to Carmen. At first she seemed to feel the same, but toward morning they did man-age one fierce coupling before separating to their own bedrolls again. To Doc, it was an oddly upsetting experience, almost like saying goodbye. He remained awake until the dim morning light began to show.

It was the middle of the day before the storm had abated enough for them to start out again. Raider cursed when he saw that the heavy rain had washed away the trail he'd been following for so long. "Ain't no way to tell how far ahead they are," he said worriedly.

Still, the general lie of the land guided them. There were not many other routes the men they were following could have taken.

"Wish I could see a little farther ahead," Raider groused, looking around at the jagged rocky land they were riding through. "Why, hell, we could ride right into the middle of 'em without hardly knowin' it."

"You already have, partner," a voice suddenly sang out from behind a clump of boulders.

Raider spun around, his hand reaching for the butt of his rifle. "Don't try it!" another voice called from the opposite direction.

Raider's gun hand moved slowly forward until it was resting in plain view on the saddle horn, next to his left. There was movement in the rocks. "They got us surrounded," he murmured to Doc.

Doc, hearing that voice, had not moved, except to nudge his horse closer to Carmen's. He looked over at her. Her face was white and pinched.

Then a man walked out into the open, holding a rifle, which he kept pointed more or less at Raider. "Guess you know you still owe me a man," he said to Raider.

It was Jake Logan.

CHAPTER SEVENTEEN

The rest of Logan's band began to make their appearances, until all were standing in the open, covering Raider and Doc with their weapons. "Get on down from your nags real slow-like," Logan ordered. Doc and Raider dismounted carefully. As soon as Raider's feet hit the ground he was relieved of his Remington. It took a little longer to locate Doc's .32 in its shoulder holster.

"Now ain't this a sweet little ole popgun," one of Logan's men snickered.

Carmen was still sitting her horse. "Come on, git down," she was told. She swung down haughtily and stood facing one of Logan's men, who, grinning, began running his hands over her body.

"Animal!" she said, and slapped his face.

The man grinned. "Jus' tryin' to find out iff'n you got any weapons, honey," he said. He patted her breasts. "An' you sure as hell do."

Doc took a step forward, but the muzzle of a rifle thrust hard into his belly drove him back.

Logan grinned. "Don't figure as I know you, mister. Why the hell are you on my trail? I've met this bastard before," he said, nodding toward Raider. "But you an' the girl . . ."

Carmen drew herself up to her full height and said, "I am Carmen Mora Gonzalez."

Logan's eyes widened. "Oh yeah? Then that either answers my question or makes me think o' some new ones."

"We're not on your trail," Doc cut in. "We're after a Mexican named Gutierrez. He killed Señorita Mora's brother a few days ago, and Señorita Mora wants justice."

Logan's hard little eyes narrowed. "Yeah, could be," he muttered. "I know about the killin'. But why the hell's she got you an' this waddie along with her?"

"We're old friends. We came along to help."

A disbelieving grin twisted Logan's lips. "Sure. Just the three of you. Naw. If you was after shootin' up Gutierrez you'd have one hell of a passel o' people along with you. And they'd be Mexicans."

He looked shrewdly at Doc and Raider. "You wouldn't be after some gold, would you?"

Raider shrugged. "Hell, I'm always interested in gold. Know of any?"

"You're a real smart bastard, ain't ya?" Logan snarled. "I don't like this. Last I saw of you, you was gunnin' down one o' my boys. Now you're way the hell and gone out here, right in the middle o' somethin' that shouldn't be none o' your business."

"You heard the man," Raider insisted. "We're just after Gutierrez."

"Well, you sure as hell found him. Him and his bunch are camped just a half mile or so the other side o' that hill." He pointed toward a ridge a short distance away. "Maybe we oughta turn you over to him—see what *he's* got to say." Then he grinned. "Minus the girl, o' course. I got some real nice games I'd like to teach her. Bet she knows a lot about them kinda games already. She's got that look. Ain't I right, honey?" he asked, grinning at Carmen.

"If you think . . ." Doc snarled, taking a step toward Logan.

Logan's gun hand dropped to the butt of his .45. He was grinning, and Raider was pretty certain he meant to kill Doc. Raider was thinking of making a desperate play for the gun of the man nearest to him when he suddenly spotted a flicker of movement from a ridge top about two hundred yards away. "Hold it!" he snapped, staring up at the ridge.

The intensity of his stance froze everyone. They all knew they were in dangerous country, and all of Logan's men spun around to face in the direction Raider was looking.

"What is it?" Logan demanded.

"Ain't sure," Raider said uneasily. "Coulda been an animal. Coulda been . . . Uh-uh! There it is again! God*damn!* An Apache!"

Everyone had seen a shadowy figure dart from the cover of one big boulder to the cover of another. "You're crazy," Logan hissed. "The Apaches are up in Arizona. On some kinda government reservation. Hell, Cochise died more'n a year ago."

"He ain't the only Apache," Raider snapped back. "There's always been one hell of a lot of 'em down this way. Been driving the Mexicans crazy for centuries. Old Juh has a band somewhere in these mountains. Nidnhi branch of the Chiracahuas, and they are one *hard* bunch. Lots of Cochise's people came on down this way rather than get shut up on the reservation."

"Hell, maybe it's some o' Gutierrez's boys," one of the men said nervously. "Maybe they found out we was here an' got around behind us."

The argument was settled for good when a shot suddenly rang out from above and the man who had been speaking grunted and sprawled forward onto his face, blood pumping from a bullet hole in his back. Everyone hit the ground, groping for shelter as the jubilant war cry of an Indian bounced from rock to rock.

Raider found himself on his belly, nose to nose with Logan. "We gotta get outta here," Logan snarled.

Raider made a quick check of the terrain. "No way. Anybody who tries goin' down that trail gets it in the back. Better to hole up here an' try and hold 'em off."

"Can't do that," Logan snapped. "Gutierrez is gonna hear the shootin'. We gotta make tracks."

"Hell, he'll probably just ride away outta trouble. An' what's more dangerous anyhow? Gutierrez or them Apaches?"

"Gutierrez," Logan said grimly. He glanced longingly down the trail. "You're right," he muttered. "No way out down there."

And then his eyes grew crafty. "Not without cover, that is." he said, looking speculatively at Raider.

"Uh-uh. I'm not gonna risk my hide to save yours," Raider said heatedly.

"Don't hardly think you got much choice, pardner," Logan said, grinning. "Remember? You owe me a man. Look, we'll give you your hardware back. You get up into those rocks right over there and pin 'em down. We'll slip down the trail a piece and then cut in around behind 'em."

"Yeah. I can see you doin' that," Raider said caustically.

"Take it or leave it. At least you got a chance this way."

"We'll take it."

Some of the men were shooting up at the rocks above. Fire was coming back at them. There really wasn't much to shoot at—just dim figures that showed themselves long enough to fire and then duck back behind cover. Raider told Doc what Logan wanted them to do. Doc agreed, with one stipulation—that Carmen stay behind with them.

Logan shrugged, then grinned. "Some people'll do anything for sex," he said.

They were given their weapons, unloaded. Raider insisted on getting his bowie knife back. Then he and Doc and Carmen sprinted for the cover of the rocks Logan had pointed out to them. The Indians opened up on them as they ran, but they made it to cover behind the rocks without being hit. They stuffed ammunition into their rifles and sent lead back up at the Apaches. Carmen too.

It was while they were firing that they heard the sound of hooves pounding back down the trail. Turning, Raider saw that Logan and his remaining men had already ridden away, under cover of the fire he and Doc and Carmen were laying down.

"You think he'll double back behind the Apaches?" Doc asked as he snapped a shot at a silhouette up above.

"Naw."

Raider was proved right a few minutes later. Logan and company were out in the open now, several hundred yards away. The Indians had been surprised by the maneuver, and for a moment there was no shooting. Then Logan waved and his voice floated up to Raider. "So long, sucker," he yelled, and then, still waving, he led his men off down the trail up which the Pinkertons had so recently ridden.

"Bastard," Doc snarled.

"Yeah. Well, we knew that already. Now let's figure out how we're gonna get outta this alive."

"You think we can?" Doc asked hopefully.

Raider glanced over at Carmen, who, despite having a firm grip on her rifle, looked white and pinched. "Uh-uh," he said. "We can hold 'em off for a while . . . till we run outta ammo. I kinda hate to say it, Doc, but we better save the last three rounds for ourselves. 'Specially with her along."

Carmen obviously understood his English, because she whitened a little more, but she compressed her lips firmly and said, "I can do whatever I have to do."

That's where they had to leave it. The Indians were slowly creeping closer, dodging from rock to rock. They had seen the bulk of their intended prey ride away. They would have to be satisfied with the three remaining, and they had already seen that one was a woman. They would keep attacking until their victims could not fight back.

Raider managed to hit one of the Apaches as he rose up to fire. The man cried out hoarsely and clapped a hand to his forehead. Blood spurted from between his fingers, then he fell back out of sight. A scream of rage rose from the other Indians.

"Kinda wish I hadn't done that," Raider muttered. "They won't be satisfied now until . . ."

He left the rest unsaid, but there was little doubt as to what he meant. The Indians were closer now, and the firing was almost continuous. Doc was desperately ramming fresh cartridges into the loading slot of his Winchester when an Indian suddenly rose up in front of him. No time to bring the rifle up, and Raider was exchanging point-blank shots with another Indian. Doc looked up at the hate-filled painted face sighting down a rifle barrel straight at him, had an impression of straight, dirty black hair tied back with a band around the temples, ragged clothing, half-Indian, half-white, and he was saying goodbye to the world when a rifle blasted almost next to his ear, nearly deafening him, and the Indian spun around, screaming in pain, his rifle flying harmlessly to one side.

Doc turned. Next to him, Carmen was levering another shell into the breech of her Winchester. Her face was intent, grim, fierce. Doc wanted to thank her for saving his life, but the words seemed inadequate, and then there was no time to think, only to fight back desperately.

And then the firing in front of them slacked off, and there were no more shadowy figures darting closer. Instead, they seemed to be retreating. But why? Suddenly there was a storm of fresh firing off to one side, accompanied by the drumming of hoofbeats. A moment later a group of horsemen came into view, riding straight toward the retreating Indians.

"It's Logan!" Doc shouted jubilantly. "He's come back!"

"No," Raider shouted back. "It's Gutierrez!"

Doc glanced back toward the flats, and, sure enough, there was Logan, with his men, fading away into the distance, and when he looked up again he saw that it was Gutierrez leading the charge toward the Indians. But the Indians were fading back out of range, into rough country impassable for horses. One Apache shook his fist at Gutierrez, tried a shot, missed, then disappeared.

There was nothing the Pinkertons could do but sit and wait for Gutierrez and his men to ride up to them. They were almost out of ammunition, and fighting was out of the question. Raider made sure that their rifles were leaning harmlessly against a rock when Gutierrez and his men rode into the little space they had been defending.

Gutierrez slipped smoothly from his horse, both his feet hitting the ground at once. He gave Raider a little bow. "We meet again, señor," he said. Then he took off his hat and bowed to Carmen. "Señorita," he murmured, then suddenly straightened, a look of surprise on his face. "Carmen Mora!" he burst out.

"I see you know me, señor, but I'm afraid you have the advantage of me."

"Pedro Gutierrez, at your service," he said curtly. "I remember seeing you in Mexico City . . . with your brother."

"Whom you killed," she replied without any visible show of emotion.

"Ah, so he died, then," Gutierrez said, then added, "And that is why . . . But no. You would not have followed me here with only these two. *Especially* these two if you only wanted . . . It must be the gold!"

"You may think as you will, señor."

He smiled then. "I am not paid to think, señorita. But I will take you to one who is very good at thinking."

Carmen raised her eyebrows. "And that would be?"

"Valdez."

CHAPTER EIGHTEEN

Fortunately, Logan had left their horses. Doc, Raider, and Carmen mounted and immediately rode out with Gutierrez and his men. Much to their surprise, they were allowed to keep their weapons. Gutierrez explained curtly, "We may have more trouble with the Apaches. We need every armed man we can get . . . and every woman."

Doc noticed that Gutierrez looked at Carmen when he said this. She was riding a little ahead of him, straight in the saddle, her face expressionless. Doc tried to read the expression on Gutierrez's face and could not.

"How come you busted in on our side against the Indians?" Raider asked.

Gutierrez shrugged his shoulders. "A natural reaction in these parts. The Apaches have been killing our people for centuries. I didn't know who you were, but I knew who *they* were. I also knew that the army unit hunting for them was nowhere in the vicinity, so it was up to us."

"There's usually Mexican troops around here?" Raider asked casually.

Gutierrez nodded. "Colonel Terrazas, the scourge of the Apaches. He patrols with Mexican troops and a band of Tarahumara scouts. Some day he'll clean out these mountains, but right now, with all the troubles in Mexico, he has too few men. But later . . . Well, Valdez may be able to do something about it."

There was little more conversation, even though both Doc and Raider tried to pump Gutierrez about Valdez. He refused to be drawn out. They rode on like that for the rest of the day, the two Pinkertons, Carmen, and Gutierrez and his dozen men. Doc stayed as close to Carmen as he could, not because he was afraid that either Gutierrez or one of the others might harm her, but because he was afraid that she might harm Gutierrez. Her rifle butt was sticking out of its scabbard only inches from her right hand, and he had seen over the past few days how driven she was by a lust for revenge against those who had killed her brother.

As for himself and Raider, neither one of them had the slightest thought of shooting their way out. They were on their way to Valdez, perhaps not as independently as they might have liked, but it was better than nothing. Doc had a vivid mental image of Carmen jerking her rifle out of its saddle scabbard and opening up on Gutierrez, and successful or not, herself being cut down in a hail of lead from Gutierrez's men.

But as the hours wore on she made no move toward her rifle. When she wasn't looking straight ahead, she was casting quick little glances Gutierrez's way. Doc saw Gutierrez meet her eyes once and hold her gaze for a few seconds. There was a considerable interplay between those two wary gazes. What the hell are they thinking about? Doc wondered.

A couple of hours before dark, Gutierrez's party turned up a narrow trail that branched off the main one. Another hour and the trail narrowed even more, passing between a cut in between sheer cliffs. A man with a rifle suddenly appeared from behind a boulder a few feet above them. Another appeared on the other side of the defile, both men covering the little cavalcade, their stance tense until they recognized Gutierrez. Then there was a hearty greeting, a wave, and they were allowed to ride on through.

"Damn! You could hold off an army here," Raider muttered to Doc. The path wound underneath sheer cliffs with good cover above.

Another half hour and Valdez's headquarters came into view. Raider made a quick appraisal of the terrain. Loaded with good defensive positions. Even if someone got this far, they'd have to fight every step of the way to get farther.

Valdez himself met them as they rode up to the main house. Doc was particularly tense. This might be the moment Carmen went for the rifle. After all, they were both here now—the man who had killed her brother and the man who had sent him. But Carmen merely dismounted when they reached the wide veranda that ran around the sides of the big house. Gutierrez went straight to Valdez, who was looking with interest at the three newcomers. A brief explanation from Gutierrez, with quick questions from Valdez, none of which either Raider or Doc could quite hear from where they were standing, and then Valdez was coming toward them.

"Welcome to my humble home," he said, accompanying his greeting with a politician's smile. He bent over Carmen's hand. "My condolences concerning your brother, señorita," he murmured. "Manuel and I were once very close."

Yeah, sure, Raider thought. That's why you sent your gunslinger to kill him.

Carmen let Valdez kiss her hand, her face still expressionless. "Yes, Manuel spoke of you often," was all she said.

Further introductions were made. Valdez digested Raider and Doc's names, then, smiling, said, "With the Pinkerton Detective Agency, of course."

He laughed at the evident surprise on the two Pinkertons' faces. "I have my sources of information. You two are perhaps more famous than you think. Tell me. Are you here because of the gold?"

Raider said nothing, but Doc saw no reason to pretend. "Of course," he said. "The bank is anxious to get their money back."

Valdez nodded. "They would be. It's amazing how many people are eager to have that gold. But I think that your English bank is not going to see any of it. It is a part of Mexico now, as it should have been from the start. But . . . come inside. You have obviously had a long and tedious journey. You will want to refresh yourselves."

Within fifteen minutes, Doc, Raider, and Carmen were being given the same first-class treatment that Manuel Mora had received that first time he had come to Valdez's valley so many years before. While Raider luxuriated in a hot bath,

Doc bathed hurriedly and was soon out in the hallway in clean clothes, looking for Carmen. However, one of Valdez's armed retainers intercepted him before he'd gone very far and took him to Valdez.

Valdez was in the big living room, talking to Gutierrez. Doc tried to make out a few words of what they were saying before they saw him coming but was unable to do so. "Ah, Dr. Weatherbee," Valdez said, rising. "We were just winding up some business. Please, come and join me in a glass of brandy. Gutierrez will be leaving."

Doc noticed that Gutierrez had not made that decision for himself. He thought he detected a slight resentment on Gutierrez's part, but Gutierrez obediently backed away and, after giving a brief little nod of his head, left the room.

"A good strong right arm," Valdez said, nodding in Gutierrez's direction. "But not the kind you'd want to share a glass of good brandy with."

What amazed Doc was that Valdez did not wait for his "good strong right arm" to completely withdraw from the room before saying this. Doc was certain Gutierrez had heard, but his face, impassive as usual, betrayed nothing. Then he was gone.

Valdez proved talkative. He was telling Doc the history of Maximilian's gold, now Valdez's gold, when Raider came into the room, followed shortly after by Carmen. Valdez had provided her with a dress, and a very fine one, and she was very beautiful as she came into the room. Doc's breath caught in his throat. He had been struck by her beauty the very first time he'd seen her, at her brother's ranch, but now, knowing so well the even greater beauty concealed beneath her clothing, he was overwhelmed. Mine. She could be mine, he thought desperately.

A sumptuous dinner was served for the four of them. Valdez talked on and on, seemingly oblivious to the natural antipathy that divided him from the others. Doc began to wonder if the man were quite sane.

Valdez began to talk of politics. "The time is coming,"

he said, "when Mexico will once again need a strong man to guide her. It is no secret that President Lerdo is not that man."

"Why is that?" Doc asked.

"My good man! The country is falling apart. Revolt everywhere. A score of petty generals ready to make their moves. Only a few with any real chance, though."

"Such as Díaz?" Doc prompted.

Valdez smiled. "I see you know something of our Mexican politics, Dr. Weatherbee. Yes, Díaz. *If* he can get the correct backing. He . . . is a little short of money. They are all a little short of money."

"But you aren't, are you?" Doc replied.

"Thanks to the unintended generosity of the English bank . . . no. However, you are not the only ones after my gold."

Seeing Doc's raised eyebrows, Valdez continued. "That man both you and Gutierrez told me about. Logan. He has to be Díaz's man."

"A gringo?"

"Why not? Díaz has been recruiting thugs from Tennessee and Arkansas, mostly Irish Americans with names like Logan. The United States government winks at this; they secretly back Díaz. Lerdo is fanatically anti-American, you know. He has been resisting for years the building of a railroad north to the border. He is a firm believer in the old saying: 'Poor Mexico—so far from God and so near to the United States.' He intends to maintain our northern deserts as a barrier between the two countries, and your government does not like that. Your businessmen see opportunity here in Mexico—if a strong leader can bring peace to our poor land."

"And that strong leader . . . ?"

"Will be me, of course. It's amazing how transferable the power of gold is. I am about to buy the services of one of the government's generals—along with his entire army. And there will still be so much of the gold left over."

"Unless Díaz gets to it first."

Valdez's face hardened. "He won't. It would take more men than he presently has to force his way in here. By the time he has enough men, it will be too late."

Doc raised his glass. The brandy was very fine. "To the next president of Mexico."

Beaming, Valdez drank, not noticing, or not choosing to notice, that Doc had not specifically mentioned any one name.

All during the meal Carmen had been quiet, polite, the very epitome of a cultured young woman. Valdez hardly paid her any attention. Doc wondered if he remembered that it was his man, Gutierrez, who had so recently killed her brother.

Over the next few days Doc began to wonder if *Carmen* remembered. The three of them, she and Doc and Raider, were more or less free to roam about the immediate vicinity of the house. They had been politely asked to refrain from wearing their arms, which request they complied with. More than once Doc noticed Carmen watching Gutierrez. And Gutierrez watching her. At first Doc thought they were carefully sizing each other up for the kill. After all, they should be natural enemies.

But then he began to wonder. There was something about the way Carmen was looking at Gutierrez. Something familiar. And then, with a peculiar lurch deep in his guts, Doc realized what it was. Those looks were so much like the looks that Carmen had given him when he had first arrived at Rancho La Libertad. No! It wasn't possible! Not with Gutierrez! The man had killed her brother! Carmen had sworn revenge!

But those looks. It became increasingly difficult to mistake what they meant—particularly to Gutierrez. The man was beginning to look confused whenever he came near the girl. Doc could understand that. He remembered his own reactions under that humid, big-eyed treatment.

He attempted to catch Carmen alone, to talk to her, but she carefully avoided him. He had not had the chance to say more than a few polite words to her since they had arrived in Valdez's valley. Doc felt the sickening hand of jealousy squeezing his insides. My God, anyone but Gutierrez!

Gutierrez himself was obviously undergoing stresses of his own, and not only because of Carmen's unexpected behavior. As jealous as Doc was growing of Gutierrez, Gutierrez was growing equally jealous of Doc, and the reason was Valdez. Valdez spent all the time he could with Doc, engaging him in animated conversations on philosophy, politics, and the arts. As he had done with Mora years before, he candidly confessed to Doc how starved he was for cultivated company.

"The men are loyal," he said, once again within Gutierrez's hearing. "Like faithful dogs, but a gentleman does not share his innermost thoughts with dogs."

Doc began to become aware that Gutierrez hated him. Fine, he thought, maybe he'll go for me and I can kill the bastard. He knew this was foolish thinking, that it was all because of Carmen, but he could not help himself. He began to follow Carmen, trying to see if she was meeting Gutierrez alone. He became short-tempered . . . obsessed.

"What the hell's the matter with you, Doc?" Raider muttered to him one day when they were alone. "We gotta be makin' some plans to get hold o' that gold an' get outta here."

They had discussed this before. The dying Mora, recounting the story of his last few years, had described as well as he could the location of the cave containing the gold. Raider figured it was about a mile away, on the other side of a low ridge that led up toward rugged hills at the back of the valley. He did not know the exact location, of course, but thought he could find it if had some time to poke around. The trouble was, despite the comforts of their captivity, Valdez's men were watching them all the time.

"We'll have to wait for an opportunity to crop up," Doc said. Raider snarled something about *making* an opportunity, but by then Doc had walked away, his mind returning to his obsession with Carmen and Gutierrez.

That obsession nearly deteriorated into madness two nights later, when, finally deciding that he would corner Carmen alone whether she liked it or not, he walked quietly down the hall in the middle of the night toward her room, which was on the far side of the house. His hand was on her doorknob and he was ready to softly call her name when he realized she was not alone in her room.

Doc's hand froze on the knob. Rage boiled up inside him. He was certain he had heard a man's voice mingled with Carmen's lighter contralto. For a moment he was ready to throw open the door and charge inside, but he held back. What if it was just a servant, bringing her something? But . . . at this time of night?

Remembering that Carmen's room had an outside window that reached nearly to the ground, Doc moved swiftly down the hall toward the back door. He knew he was acting like a fool, that if the girl had a man in her room, it would be best to leave and perhaps face her with it tomorrow. But he couldn't. A sick jealousy spurred him on as he silently approached the window. He slid along the wall, slowly moving his head into position next to the window frame, not wanting to see what he knew he would see, but perversely, *having* to see.

There was one small lamp lit inside Carmen's room, providing a dim golden glow. Enough of a glow so that he could make out the rich sheen of Carmen's naked flesh. She was lying on her back on her bed, a man bending over her, partly naked, his face silhouetted against the lamplight. Gutierrez!

Doc watched the man's hands violate the breasts of the woman Doc loved. He nearly choked with rage, nearly went over the sill and into the room shouting, but a last vestige of common sense stopped him. He had never yet seen Gutierrez without a gun within easy reach. His first move into that room would very likely be his last, unless he too were armed.

Doc slipped away from the window and then broke into a run toward the back door and the hallway and his room, where his .32 lay hidden in the bottom of a drawer. However, a guard, seeing a running man heading for the house, called out a loud warning and ordered him to halt. Cursing, Doc did so; he knew that Valdez's men were quick on the trigger.

The guard demanded to know what he was doing outside. Doc tried to make up a story, keeping his voice low, wishing the guard would do the same. He heard movement from inside the house. Damn! It must be Gutierrez, leaving Carmen's room. He wanted to push the guard aside, rush into his room, get his pistol, and kill Gutierrez before he could get away.

But, too late. While the guard was detaining him he heard the front door open and close and knew that Gutierrez would be gone. He would be ready now, if Doc came after him. With difficulty, Doc finally managed to satisfy the guard that he had merely gone out of the house to urinate. The guard, grumbling, let him inside again. Doc went straight to his room and took out his pistol. But he did not follow Gutierrez. He would take care of Gutierrez later. First he had to decide if he wanted to kill Carmen, too.

Over the next couple of days he was unable to hide from Carmen the fact that he knew. His expression as he looked at her was a dead giveaway. She studiously avoided him. He saw Gutierrez once, but the man left before he could approach. The only thing holding Doc back from forcing the issue was Raider. Any wild action on Doc's part would endanger his partner.

So he missed his chance. Late one morning Doc was awakened by sounds of shouting. Quickly pulling on his clothes, he ran out into the hall and followed the sounds to the front veranda, where he found Valdez, wildly excited, issuing orders to a number of his men. It was only after they had ridden away in the direction of the entrance to the valley that Valdez finally turned toward Doc.

"That filthy traitor!" Valdez snarled, staring right through

Doc as if he were not there.

"What's the matter? What's happened?" Doc demanded.

"Gutierrez!" Valdez half screamed. "He's deserted! They're gone! They're both gone!"

An awful possibility was beginning to occur to Doc. "Who's gone?" he half whispered.

"Gutierrez. And that whore—Carmen Mora."

CHAPTER NINETEEN

Doc's face felt very hot. Carmen . . . gone with Gutierrez. For a few seconds he became oblivious to everything around him, able to think only of the obscenity of Carmen being with the man who had become his enemy. Only gradually did he become aware that Valdez was speaking to him.

Doc shook himself, tried to bring his emotions under some kind of control. He saw that Valdez was looking at him shrewdly. "Ah, yes," Valdez murmured. "I see that you . . . are not particularly pleased by what has happened."

By now, Raider, alerted by all the activity, had arrived. "What the hell's goin' on?" he demanded of Doc.

"It's Carmen," Doc replied woodenly. "She's run off with Gutierrez."

"Oh, is that all?" Raider replied, for which Doc hated him.

"No, that is *not* all," Valdez broke in. "Gutierrez is fully aware that, to me, what he has done is an act of treachery, and knowing how I will respond to that, he will be ready for even more treachery. He can cause great damage. Gutierrez knows so much about . . . about my plans."

Raider's steady gaze held Valdez's agitated one. "Guess you better get the hell after him, then."

"It's not that easy," Valdez said heatedly. "If I send my men out to track him down, I will leave myself shorthanded here. And without knowing where Díaz is . . ."

"Porfirio Díaz is here?"

"I don't know. He's sold his interest in La Candelaria, his sugar plantation. I have word that he's told everyone he's going to try his hand at ranching in Durango—which lies in this general direction. But with his man, Logan, having followed Gutierrez's trail for so long . . ."

"Yeah, I see what you mean," Raider said.

"However," Valdez said silkily, "I can see that your friend, Dr. Weatherbee, is quite upset about Gutierrez and Señorita

Mora. I suspect that he may have as much desire as I to apprehend them."

Doc, recovering from his first shock, was becoming more and more aware of the conversation between Raider and Valdez. Hope leaped inside him. "I want to go after them," he managed to grate out.

"My idea exactly," Valdez said, smiling. "How long will it take you to get ready?"

"Fifteen minutes," Raider answered for Doc. "Just enough time to get our gear together and stock up on some supplies."

"Your horses will be saddled and waiting," Valdez said.

Doc and Raider went straight to their respective rooms. The first thing Doc did was fasten the shoulder rig for his .32. Scooping up the rest of his gear, he beat Raider to where Valdez was waiting with their horses.

Valdez looked into Doc's eyes, his own little eyes as hard as flint. "Kill him for me," he hissed to Doc. "Kill Gutierrez. What you do with the girl is your own affair."

Raider came into view, lugging his saddlebags and rifle. Doc nodded to Valdez and mounted. A couple of minutes later he and Doc were cantering away from the house, accompanied by one of Valdez's men, who would help them follow Gutierrez and Carmen's trail.

They went out through the valley's main pass. Raider noticed that there were extra men guarding the entrance, and that everyone seemed particularly tense. "I'd sure hate to hafta get in here today," Raider said to Doc. "Damn place is stirred up worse'n a pissed-on ant's nest."

Doc said nothing. He sat his horse rigidly, staring straight ahead, his mind full of images of Gutierrez and Carmen. He remembered the sight of Gutierrez's hands on Carmen's breasts. His right hand drifted toward the butt of his revolver under his jacket. His fingers touched the smooth wood.

Raider rode up close to him. "Doc," he said sharply. "You're actin' like an asshole. I know the girl means a lot to you, but damn it, we got a job to do. Snap out of it before you git the both of us killed."

The words cut through Doc's obsession like a whip. He

shook his head, trying to clear his mind. It was easier now that they were away from the valley, just himself and Raider and Valdez's man. As they rode, he began to realize how confused his thoughts had been ever since arriving at Mora's ranch, ever since coming under Carmen's spell. The air of unreality inside Valdez's valley had not helped. "You're right," he said curtly.

The thought of Carmen in Gutierrez's arms still filled him with anger and loathing, but he was now able to put the whole thing in a little better perspective. Face it, Weatherbee, he told himself. You win some, you lose some. He'd still kill Gutierrez if he got the chance, but not just because of Carmen. The killing of Manuel Mora was reason enough for Gutierrez to die. Doc had liked Mora. As for Carmen . . . better not to think about her for the time being. "I'll be all right," he said to Raider.

They rode on for the rest of the day. Valdez's man did most of the tracking, not that Gutierrez and the girl had done much to conceal their trail, but the farther they rode, the more nervous the Mexican became. "I wish we had more men," he muttered.

They rode into trouble about an hour before sundown. It was a cold clear day. Sound traveled far. They were riding toward a little pass when Raider heard the neighing of a horse. "That's damned close!" he snapped.

He was about to wheel his mount when a line of horsemen appeared on top of a little rise about fifty yards away. Raider glanced to the rear. Boxed in. More horsemen were riding in behind them. He and Doc froze, but Valdez's man spun his horse and spurred it toward a small side canyon. "Don't try it!" Raider shouted, but too late. He heard the sharp report of a rifle from the ridge above, where the line of horsemen were, and a bullet knocked the Mexican from his saddle. The man hit hard, rolled, and came to a stop in a sitting position. He sat there for a moment, then lurched groggily to his feet, jerking out his revolver. Another shot and he was slammed over onto his back. This time he did not rise.

Doc looked up at the ridge. One of the riders held a still-smoking rifle. It was Gutierrez. Doc was tempted to charge him, although he knew he didn't have a chance, not with all those men up there. Better to wait until the bastard made a mistake and then take him out.

If Gutierrez gave him the chance. His rifle barrel swung toward Doc. Doc braced himself for the blow of a bullet, but suddenly an authoritative voice rang out and Doc saw the muzzle of Gutierrez's rifle waver. Another, sharper command, and Gutierrez slowly and reluctantly slid his rifle back into its saddle scabbard.

A tall man on a big white horse rode out a little in front of the other horsemen. Both Doc and Raider saw him say something to Gutierrez. They couldn't make out the words, but Gutierrez didn't seem to like them. His face hardened, and he said something back, but the tall man cut him off with an abrupt gesture. The other horsemen began to close in around Gutierrez, and he quickly shut up. The tall man stared hard at him for a few seconds, then, turning his horse, he rode slowly toward Doc and Raider.

The two Pinkertons sat their horses, unmoving, careful to keep their hands away from their weapons. The tall man stopped his mount in front of them. "My apologies for such poor behavior," he said, "but that man is not one of mine."

"We know," Doc said. "And I have a score to settle with him."

The tall man smiled. "I think he feels the same way about you. However, I do not permit personal vendettas when they come into conflict with my plans."

"Your plans?"

The tall man hesitated, then smiled. It was quite a nice smile, a flashing of white teeth below the thick black drooping mustache that bisected the tall man's face. However, the smile did not quite reach his eyes. They were Indian eyes set into an olive face, obsidian black, tilted up a little at the corners. "Permit me to introduce myself," the man said. "I am Porfirio Díaz."

"Ah, General Díaz," Doc said. "We have heard so much about you."

"And I about you . . . from Gutierrez. I understand you were with Manuel Mora."

"Until Gutierrez killed him."

Díaz's eyebrows raised. "He didn't tell me that."

"And I doubt he wanted me to live long enough to bring you the news."

Díaz nodded, and his eyes were hard. "Then that is a debt that remains to be collected. However, as I have told you, I do not permit personal grievances to interfere with the smooth running of a campaign. At the moment I need Gutierrez. There will be time later . . . But wait! Mora's sister is with Gutierrez!"

"Yes, I know," Doc said icily.

Díaz's eyes grew thoughtful. "This is all very confusing. I would not have though her the kind of woman to be with her brother's assassin. But never mind. That is something to worry about another day. First, we will get down to today's work."

"Which is . . . ?"

"To take Valdez."

"And the gold."

Díaz looked straight at Doc. "Yes, the gold. I know why you and your partner are here, Dr. Weatherbee. See? Gutierrez has at least told me your names. But I must warn you, that gold is mine. You may ride with me if you care to, but do not think to cheat me."

Beneath Díaz's surface politeness Doc detected a remorseless iron will ready to make itself known at any moment. He shuddered. No, he would not like to have this man for an enemy.

Raider broke in. "You hitting Valdez today?"

"Yes. Gutierrez says that he knows a weakly defended point. That is why he is useful to me. Would you care to join our assault?"

Raider and Doc looked at one another. They nodded.

"Yeah," Raider said to Díaz.

Díaz laughed. "Good. It's better this way, because I would not have allowed you to ride away from here on your own. Not with what you know."

Doc made no comment. He did wonder, however, if Díaz intended that they *ever* ride away. At the moment there was no choice, so Raider and Doc rode back with Díaz toward the line of horsemen on top of the rise. The others, those who had gotten around behind them, came jingling after. Raider saw that all Díaz's men were well armed, with the latest repeating rifles, revolving pistols, plus swords and machetes. They looked highly capable.

Gutierrez stared stonily at Doc when he, Raider, and Díaz rode up. Doc stared back just as stonily. Then he saw Carmen, sitting her horse about twenty yards away. When he looked at her she quickly looked away.

Another man rode out of the main group and headed toward Raider. Jake Logan. "You're sure one hell of a lucky dude," he said, grinning. "Last time I saw you, you was entertainin' a bunch o' 'Paches, an' havin' one helluva time of it."

"Well, hello, yella-belly," Raider said pleasantly.

Logan paled. "Watch your mouth, cousin," he said in a low, cold voice.

"Sure you got enough men backin' you, snake-shit?" Raider asked, his voice still pleasant but his eyes cold.

Logan's right hand dropped toward the butt of his pistol, but Díaz suddenly rode in between him and Raider. "If either one of you causes trouble, I will have you shot," he snapped. Both Raider and Logan refused to take their eyes off each other, but they reluctantly nodded agreement when Díaz demanded, more loudly, "Do you understand?"

They set off then, Díaz's little army. Raider estimated that there were about two hundred men. That sounded like good odds against the maybe fifty that Valdez had, until Raider reviewed in his mind the series of good defensive positions that protected Valdez's headquarters. Even if Díaz made it into the valley, the land would be fighting on Valdez's side.

They rode through half the night, finally stopping just a couple of miles short of the main pass into the valley. The men were permitted to sleep for a while, or to eat, or pray—whatever each man felt he needed. The leaders went over the final plans for the assault.

"About half the men are going to pin down the guards at the main pass," Díaz explained to Raider. The general's knack for singling out men of military ability had drawn him to the big Pinkerton. "Then," he added, "Gutierrez is going to lead the other half around behind a weak point, over a path he knows about but few others do. Once through, that group will swing around behind the main pass and trap the defenders. The rest of the action will consist of mopping up."

Raider nodded. "Lucky Gutierrez came your way when he did. We had a man like him in our country once—name of Benedict Arnold. He wasn't too popular."

"Of course not," Díaz replied, his face serious. "Nor do I trust him. If he is willing to betray Valdez, he will perhaps someday be willing to betray me. Perhaps even today. That is why I would like to ask you to ride with his group."

"To see he don't stab you in the back? But what makes you think *I* ain't gonna do the same, General?"

Díaz smiled again, that smile that didn't quite reach his eyes. "Because, at that moment, it would not be to your advantage," he said. "At least, not until we're inside the valley. Then . . . we will see."

Raider grinned. "Okay, we'll play it your way."

But Raider had his doubts. He thought that Díaz might be underestimating Valdez. But no point in saying too much. Let the two of them chop each other up. He was still working for the Pinkerton National Detective Agency.

The little army was getting ready to ride off in its two separate directions when Doc noticed that Carmen was getting ready to mount up with the rest. He could not believe that she was going, or that Díaz would permit it, but the general didn't even seem to notice. Doc looked hard at Carmen. Face to face he could not hate her. He started to walk over to her, but then stiffened when he saw that Gutierrez was already approaching the girl. Doc tried to look away, but could not.

He saw Gutierrez reach out for Carmen. Then, to Doc's surprise—and evidently to Gutierrez's, too—she pushed his hand away. Gutierrez recoiled, then said something. Carmen snapped something back, and Gutierrez abruptly spun on his heel and walked away. There was only the dim light of a small fire to see by, but Doc saw that the man's face was rigid with anger. Doc tried to make out the expression on Carmen's face, but the light was coming from the wrong direction.

Then Díaz gave the order and it was time to mount up and move out. Doc and Raider went with Gutierrez's group, as planned. Doc was glad that Logan was riding with Díaz and the main group. Otherwise there'd be trouble between him and Raider. Not that he himself was in much of a better situation with Gutierrez so close. He'd have to watch his back. At least they had left Carmen behind.

They had ridden about a mile before he realized that Carmen was with them after all. She had ridden up from behind. Gutierrez said something to Díaz's man leading the attack force, but the man refused to send the girl back. "It's too late," he insisted. "If she wants to get shot, that's her business."

So Carmen continued along with them, riding fairly close to Gutierrez but not looking at him.

What the hell is going on between them? Doc wondered. A faint hope began to flicker inside him.

It was just beginning to grow light when they reached the small path the Gutierrez claimed would take them around behind the defenders of one of the smaller passes. About twenty men were left to hit this pass from the front, to create a diversion. The rest of the group started up the path, making every attempt to maintain silence, and were relatively successful. Once, a horse stumbled and a man cursed, but otherwise, there was little noise.

Then, from a distance, heavy firing broke out. The detachment under Díaz was attacking the main pass, pinning down the bulk of Valdez's men. A few minutes later there was firing from much closer. The twenty men had gone into action against the lesser pass.

For Gutierrez's group, the going was painfully slow. The narrowness of the trail would only permit them to ride single-file, and there were eighty men. It was full daylight before they reached the end of the trail, although the sun had not yet risen above the mountaintops. The trail dumped them out onto a little plain behind the small pass the twenty were attacking. From here they could clearly see the defenders huddling behind boulders, their backs to them. Gutierrez attempted to point out the best way to attack, but there was no need. It was quite clear from the lie of the land what needed to be done. The commander contemptuously brushed aside Gutierrez's suggestions; Gutierrez was already beginning to reap a traitor's reward.

The charge was short and sharp, taking the defenders from two sides. There were only a half-dozen men to be disposed of, and those who were not instantly killed barely managed to slip away and hide in the rocks.

It was now time for the main action. The twenty rode in through the little pass that had just been cleared, joining the eighty already inside the valley, and then the entire hundred men swept around in a big arc, ready to take the defenders of the main pass from the rear.

It did not turn out to be that easy. The rest of Valdez's men had heard shooting from behind them and, leaving a suicide guard at the pass to slow Díaz, fell back toward Valdez's main headquarters. As Raider had foreseen, Valdez's men were making good use of the terrain and the secondary defensive positions. There was no question now of simply charging in and mopping up. It was going to be a hard, slogging fight.

Díaz had also assessed the situation and was deploying

his men accordingly. A damn good general, Raider thought, impressed by Díaz's tactics. Spendthrift with his men's lives, though. The men, however, fought as they were ordered, steadily pushing back Valdez's men. Díaz himself had no hesitation about placing himself in the hottest part of the fight.

Raider himself held back. He had no particular reason to kill any of Valdez's men. He was watching the fight from about two hundred yards back when he remembered that he had not seen Doc for a few minutes. He turned, looking for his partner, and then saw him a few hundred yards away, galloping after a pair of riders. "Oh shit," Raider muttered, spurring his horse in that direction. That pair of riders was Gutierrez and Carmen.

Doc had also been staying back out of the fighting, but instead of watching the flow of battle, he had been keeping an eye on Carmen. She was sitting her horse some ways off when Doc saw Gutierrez ride up to her. The two engaged in an animated conversation for some time. Gutierrez obviously trying to convince Carmen of something. She finally nodded, and the two of them rode off on an oblique line that would take them far to one side of the fighting. Doc instantly spurred his mount after them.

Carmen and Gutierrez, riding hard, disappeared over the brow of a hill. Doc, anxious not to lose them, was incautious, and almost rode straight into them. They had stopped their horses in the middle of a wide spot in the trail, just on the other side of the little hill, and were looking down at the ranch house, which was about a quarter of a mile away. The trail they were on led around to the side, far from the house and past it, toward the back of the valley.

Doc had time to see that much, and then he had to pull his horse back on its haunches to keep it from crashing into Gutierrez and Carmen's mounts, and while he was still trying to recover his balance, he realized that Gutierrez had gone for his gun. No chance to go for his, not enough time. Fortunately, Gutierrez did not shoot immediately.

"You came after her like a fly to honey," Gutierrez said,

grinning over the muzzle of his revolver. The hammer had already been cocked. Doc was a few ounces of finger-pressure away from being dead.

Doc held himself completely motionless. He noticed that Carmen had backed her horse farther down the trail, and that was bad. She was now behind Gutierrez, which meant that if Doc opened up on Gutierrez, he might hit Carmen. Not that it mattered much. Gutierrez would cut him down before he even got his hand inside his jacket.

Doc's eyes followed the path. It obviously led to the ridge that had so interested Raider. The ridge that he believed hid the cave Mora had told them about. "You're going after the gold," he said flatly to Gutierrez.

"Of course. After I've killed you."

Doc looked to the left, then stiffened. "You're not the only one. Valdez is making a try for it too."

He had spotted several men and what appeared to be a string of pack animals racing away from the embattled house. He doubted that they would be visible from where Díaz was attacking. Gutierrez started to turn his head and look, which was what Doc was hoping for, but he abruptly jerked his head around to the front. His pistol rose. Doc realized that the man intended to shoot him first and then look. He desperately twisted to one side, going for his gun, knowing that a gunman as good as Gutierrez would get him anyhow.

There was a combined roar of two shots firing almost simultaneously. Doc flinched, expecting the impact of a bullet, but it was his horse that screamed in pain. As the animal reared, Doc saw Gutierrez falling from the saddle. He couldn't understand why—he hadn't even gotten his gun out of its holster. And then he saw Carmen riding forward, her rifle in her hands, smoke curling from its barrel.

Gutierrez had landed on his back. He tried to sit up, but couldn't. Carmen nearly straddled him with her horse's legs. He still had his pistol in his hand and tried to bring it up. Carmen pointed her rifle down at him. "This is for Manuel," she cried out, "and for the touch of your filthy body."

She fired, the bullet taking Gutierrez in the middle of the chest. His body arched spasmodically, then fell back, motionless. Doc was unable to do anything but watch; his horse, hit by Gutierrez's misdirected bullet after Carmen had shot him in the back, was toppling. Doc had only enough time to kick his feet free of the stirrups, and then he was rolling to one side, frantically trying to avoid being pinned beneath the dying animal. He was knocked breathless when he landed. He lay, gasping for air, vaguely aware of Carmen sitting her horse a few feet away, looking down at him.

"I'm sorry," she said sadly. "So sorry for it all, sorry that it could not have been different."

And then she spun her horse and raced off down the trail.

CHAPTER TWENTY

Carmen had barely disappeared around a bend in the trail when Raider rode up. His first thoughts verged on panic. He saw two men and a horse down and was certain that Doc and Gutierrez had killed one another until Doc, sucking in air, started to get shakily to his feet.

Raider was off his horse and beside Doc in a second. "Where you hit?" he demanded.

"Nowhere," Doc managed to grunt. "He got my horse. Carmen got him."

"Carmen?"

"Yes. I've been wrong about her, Raider. I think she got close to Gutierrez just so she could get him off his guard and then kill him. And probably Valdez, too. Damn! We've got to get after her. She's gone for Valdez."

Raider finally managed to get Doc to slow down enough to explain about having seen Valdez riding away from the ranch house and toward the cave containing the gold. Valdez had long ago passed out of sight, but now, as the two Pinkertons looked down from their vantage point, they could see a solitary rider racing along the trail over which Valdez had so recently passed.

"Carmen," Doc said. "Come on. We've got to stop her."

He leaped aboard Gutierrez's horse, which, like the well-trained war-horse it was, had been standing patiently by despite all the shooting. With Raider a few lengths behind, Doc pounded down the trail, wanting desperately to reach Carmen before she caught up with Valdez.

They had nearly reached the little canyon that contained the cave before Raider finally succeeded in urging a little caution on Doc. Once they had passed the ridge that Raider believed screened the canyon from the rest of the valley, they rode very carefully, looking for sign, listening. Finally, they heard voices ahead and, dismounting, covered the last hundred yards on foot.

Sliding forward on their bellies, Doc and Raider cautiously peered over a small rise. The little canyon lay below them. The brush that normally concealed the mouth of the cave had been pushed aside. To Doc's dismay, he saw that Carmen had already reached the cave. She stood below him, facing Valdez. There were four other men present, loading the last of the gold onto the mules. That is, three of them were. The fourth was holding Carmen's rifle and obviously standing guard over her.

Carmen and Valdez were arguing. Since Doc and Raider were only about forty yards away, they could hear every word.

"You bitch!" Valdez was snarling. "You've ruined everything for me."

"Good," she replied coolly. "I'm glad that you are ruined. My only regret is that I have not yet killed you. I shot Gutierrez, did I tell you that? He's lying dead back down the trail. I killed him with my brother's rifle, that one right there that your man is holding. My brother is half avenged, Valdez."

Valdez seemed stunned. "You say you killed Gutierrez?" he demanded. "After seducing him away from me?"

She laughed. "I seduced him, yes—to use him against you. But it was really you who drove him into Díaz's arms, with your arrogance, your insane pride. Ugh! To think I let that animal touch me!"

As fascinated as Doc was by the conversation below, he nevertheless knew something was going to have to be done very quickly. He and Raider could not just open up on the five men. Carmen was very likely to be hit in the crossfire. He was turning toward Raider to try and outline a plan when developments below tipped over the edge into disaster. Valdez had just insisted he would have the last laugh. After all, he was saving both his life and the gold.

"Ha!" Carmen said derisively. "You will never make it. There were others following me down the trail to this canyon. They should be here at any moment."

She turned suddenly, pointing toward the mouth of the canyon. "See? There they are now."

Everyone turned toward where she was pointing, including Doc and Raider, everyone expecting to see a platoon of Díaz's men riding into view. But it was only a ruse. With everyone's attention diverted, Carmen suddenly tried to take her rifle away from the man holding it. She managed to surprise him enough to get the stock and action into her hands, but the startled guard desperately held onto the barrel, which cost him his life, because the muzzle was now pointing straight at him. Carmen pulled the trigger, sending a bullet into the man's body, blasting him away from the gun barrel.

Now that she had full possession of the rifle, she turned back toward Valdez, levering another cartridge into the barrel. But Valdez was too quick for her. "Bitch!" he screamed and, producing a small revolver, shot her point-blank in the chest.

Carmen staggered backwards, the rifle discharging, blasting gravel from around Valdez's feet. He might have fired at her again, but, crying out in horror and rage, Doc suddenly rose up on top of his little hill and began firing at the men below. His first shot missed Valdez, who, looking up in terror, leaped for cover behind some bushes. And then the remaining three men were firing at Doc and he had to fire back at them to stay alive. He hit one on his next shot, while Raider dropped a second. The third man tried to make it into the safety of the cave mouth, but both Doc and Raider hit him before he could get inside.

A second later Doc was sliding down the slippery side of the canyon, desperate to reach Carmen. She lay on her back, still holding the rifle. He could see her hands moving, trying to work the action again, but she was too weak. He reached her side, bent over her, gently taking the rifle. "Carmen," he murmured, horrified as he watched blood welling up in the center of her chest, soaking the fabric of her blouse.

For the first time Carmen became aware of who it was bending over her. "Doc," she murmured. "Did . . . did you get him?"

"Who?"

"Valdez."

Doc looked up. Raider was checking the bodies of the four men who'd been shot for signs of life. From farther up the canyon he could hear the sound of Valdez's boots slipping and sliding over loose gravel as he tried to escape. He looked down at Carmen again. There was such fierce hope in her eyes that he could not tell her the truth—that Valdez was still alive. "Yes," he said softly. "I got him."

A look of peace came over the girl's lovely features. "It's over, then," she half whispered.

Meanwhile, Doc had been unfastening her blouse. His face paled when he bared her wound. Directly between her lovely breasts was a small hole, tinged blue around the edges, slowly pumping blood. Doc tried to tell himself that it might not be fatal. Maybe if they could get her to a doctor . . .

Carmen was speaking again. "I'm sorry . . . for what I did to you," she murmured, her voice almost inaudible. "The thing with Gutierrez. I thought it was the only way to eventually get them both. Now . . . I think it was a mistake. If only I could have . . ."

One of her hands rose slowly to his face. Her fingers gently touched his cheek. Doc seized her hand, held it tightly.

"I . . . was learning to love you," Carmen said. Then her breath escaped in a soft little sigh and Doc realized that the hand he was holding was completely limp. He looked down at Carmen, saw that her eyes were still partially open, but that they were looking at nothing. The girl was dead.

Doc gently laid her hand down on her breast, then folded the other over it. He passed his fingers over her eyelids, closing her eyes. He stood, then, staring up the canyon toward where Valdez had disappeared. *"Valdez!"* he half screamed. *"I'm coming for you!"*

He picked up Carmen's rifle, the one she said belonged to her brother. He met Raider's eyes, but his partner made no attempt to stop him.

"You want me to go with you?" was all Raider said.

Doc shook his head. Eyes cold with fury, he started up the canyon after Valdez. Raider watched him go, then began to check the pack animals. They were completely loaded and ready to travel. He was checking the last of the pack girths when he suddenly heard the sound of a horse's hooves coming from just outside the canyon. A moment later Jake Logan rode into sight. He stopped his horse and looked down at the bodies littering the ground. Then he looked at the loaded mules. "Been doin' a little prospectin', I see," he said drily.

Raider looked up at him coldly. "You here to make sure Díaz gets what he wants?"

Logan laughed. "Not on your tintype," he said as he dismounted. He was about ten yards away from Raider, standing relaxed but ready, his right hand close to the butt of his gun. "Ever since I heard about the gold," he said, "I been figurin' ways to get my hands on it. All of it, just for ole Jake Logan. An' jus' like with the Indians, I see you already done all the work for me, you poor sucker."

Raider moved his feet a little, making certain that he was standing on solid ground, that he would not slip. "Guess all you gotta do is take it away from me, Logan," was all he said.

Logan grinned. He seemed to relax for a moment, as if backing down, but Raider saw that moment when his eyes promised movement, and Raider's right hand was streaking for his gun before Logan actually moved. Jake tried to speed up his draw, which made him clumsy, and he was still cocking his .45 when the heavy slug from Raider's .44 hit him in the chest. "Oh Jesus," he gasped, reeling back from the force of the impact. He tried to backpedal, but his knees were collapsing, and he sat down hard, then fell over onto his back. Raider moved forward, kicking the pistol out of Logan's hand, but Logan's eyes were already glazing over in death. Raider stood over him for a moment. "Now I owe you *two* men, shithead," he said. "But I don't think you're gonna collect."

Meanwhile, Doc was moving quickly up the canyon. He had gone about fifty yards when he heard some more scrabbling ahead of him. Valdez was on the run again. Doc thought of Carmen, lying dead, and a stab of pure hatred went through him. "I'm on my way, Valdez," he called out.

A bullet came winging his way—nowhere close, a wild panic shot. Doc ran forward a few more yards, not making any attempt to be silent. Let the bastard know he was coming. Let him sweat.

And then he saw Valdez, slipping and sliding over loose gravel, trying to make it to the cover of some boulders. Doc halted, raising the rifle to his shoulder. He opened fire, working the lever rapidly, sending a half-dozen shots Valdez's way. Gravel flew into the air, bullets pinged off rocks. He could hear Valdez screaming, even over the sound of the shots, and then Valdez was down, clutching his right leg.

Doc raced forward, aware that Valdez was aiming his pistol at him. "Go on, shoot, you bastard. I'll give you that much chance."

One, two, three shots from Valdez's little revolver, but his hands were shaking so badly that every shot missed, and then the pistol was empty and Doc was standing over Valdez, aiming the rifle. "No," Valdez whimpered, but Doc squeezed the trigger. A dry click was the only result. The rifle was empty.

A moment's wild hope on Valdez's face, and he was digging inside his coat for another weapon, his hand appearing with a single-shot derringer, but Doc had also reached inside his coat and now his .32 was in his hand. He fired a split second before Valdez, his bullet hitting Valdez in the shoulder, making him miss. Valdez lay on his back, bleeding, looking up into the small black hole in the muzzle of Doc's Smith and Wesson. His mouth started to form the words, "No," but Doc fired before he could speak. The bullet plowed into Valdez's chest.

"That was for Carmen," Doc said grimly. "And this one is for Manuel Mora. And the rest are for all the other people you've ground under your heel, you son of a bitch."

The bullets slammed, one after the other, into Valdez, each impact making his body jerk. He was still looking up at Doc when the hammer finally came down on an empty. One last look of horror, and Valdez was dead.

Doc looked down at the man he had just killed. His rage began to leave him. It was not a fair trade! God, he'd gladly give Valdez another hundred years to live if it would bring Carmen back. But it would not. Nothing would.

He slowly made his way back down to the cave area, reloading his pistol as he walked, Mora's rifle tucked under one arm. When he got back to the cave, Raider was dragging dead bodies from one position to another. He looked up at Doc. "You get him?"

Doc nodded. "Yes. What are you doing? Say! Isn't that Logan?"

"Yeah. He came for his share, an' I gave it to him. Right now I'm tryin' to make it look like all these dudes killed each other."

He nodded toward Carmen's body. "The only thing that don't fit in is her."

Doc looked down at the dead girl. He noticed that she had a slight smile on her face. She looked as if she were asleep and having a pleasant dream. "I'll take care of her," he said.

He gently picked her up, aware of the warmth of her flesh, but also aware that it was already cooling. He would never again feel the incredible heat of her skin when she . . . But it was better not to think about that.

He took her inside the cave, and after laying the rifle on top of her body, he stacked rocks over her. He did his best to make it look like a natural rock fall; he didn't want anybody disturbing Carmen. The work didn't take long, not more than fifteen minutes, and then Raider was calling from outside, "Come on, Doc, we gotta get outta here before anybody else shows up."

One last moment of goodbye, and then Doc joined his partner. The two of them rode out of the canyon, leading the string of gold-laden mules. It took Raider a little while to find the secret trail that Mora had described, but when he did he saw why Mora had been able to make such a clean getaway. Most of the surface was hard stone. They would leave no tracks behind them.

Off in the distance, firing was still continuing near the ranch house, but was beginning to slacken a little. In another hour at the most Díaz would be in possession of the house, and then he would begin to wonder what had happened to certain people. With luck it would take the rest of the day for him to put it all together, and by then Doc and Raider would have a considerable lead. But that lead would not last forever. With the manpower he had, Díaz still had a good chance of catching them before they made it to the border.

Like Mora earlier, they pushed themselves and their mounts for the next twenty-four hours before finally collapsing for a little sleep. On the third day they passed close enough to a town for Doc to ride in alone and send a telegram. And then they were on their way again, two mounted men and four pack mules. An attractive target for any *banditos* who might wonder what those mules carried.

A week later they were very close to the border. Out of food and water, they had no choice but to ride into a small town for supplies. It was while they were eating in a cantina that Raider spotted the trouble. "Damn it, Doc," he murmured, "I guess we ain't gonna make it."

Doc looked up to see what his partner meant, and then he too saw the half-dozen men riding down the main street straight toward the cantina. Neither he nor Raider needed formal introductions to tell them they were Díaz's men.

The six men stopped outside the cantina. One of them walked up to the mules and took a long hard look at the bulging, obviously very heavy packs. He glanced up, looking inside the cantina. The other five fanned out and followed him to the entranceway, which was nothing more than a big open archway. The leader looked straight at Raider. "I think you have something we want, señor."

Raider shrugged. "If you think you can take it."

The man smiled. "I think we can. And as for you, señor, my general has ordered me to make certain that you never have another opportunity to betray him."

Raider did not have to ask which general. Díaz had caught them after all. He was wondering who was going to make the first move when suddenly one of the Mexicans spun around and looked down the street. *"Jefe!"* he hissed. *"Problemas."*

At first Raider thought that it was part of a trick, but then he heard the sound of horses' hooves outside. A lot of horses. A minute later an American voice called out, "Raider? Doc? You in there?"

A smile split Raider's face. "In here, Jim," he sang out. He continued smiling as a group of a dozen heavily armed Americans rode up in front of the little cantina.

Díaz's man looked uncertain for a moment, but he was clearly outgunned—a dozen men behind him, Raider and Doc in front. He nodded at Doc and Raider. "Until another time, señores." And then he signaled to his men and they mounted up and rode slowly out of town.

Jim Bates dismounted and stepped inside the cantina. "The New Orleans office sent us out right after they got your telegram that you'd be comin' this way. One hell of a ride, though. God, am I dry! This place got any decent beer?"

Raider grinned. "The best in the world—an' it's on me."

EPILOGUE

An hour before, it had been raining, but as Doc rode into the mission yard, the sun was out and the ground already drying. He was surprised by how much green there was. It had been so dry when he'd been here three months before.

Only three months. So much had happened: Mora's death, the ride into Mexico, Valdez, Díaz, the return of the gold. And of course, Carmen. Before dismounting, Doc looked away to the east, up the San Luis Rey Valley, toward the mountains. Toward Rancho La Libertad.

Father William, having heard Doc's horse, came out of the mission church, still wearing the familiar brown robe that Doc had seen him in before. It took Father William a moment to place Doc's face, and then he smiled. "You're back," he said simply.

"Yes. I had a little unfinished business to take care of in these parts.

Father William's expression was pleasantly curious as he watched Doc dismount, then take the saddlebags from his horse and sling them over his shoulder. The Franciscan led Doc into his living quarters. They were quite Spartan. On the way in, Doc looked around at the crumbling facade of the old Spanish mission, as he had the first time he'd come here.

Once in the priest's room, Doc set the saddlebags down on the single big wooden table. They clinked heavily. Father William's eyes widened as Doc unfastened the flap and scooped out a pile of gleaming gold coins. "For the mission, Father," Doc said.

Father William stood speechless, staring at the gold. "On one condition only," Doc continued. "That you use part of it for a memorial to Carmen Mora somewhere in this church. I'll be riding farther east in a little while, to Pala, with a similar gift for Father Gregorio. And with the same request—that he dedicate a memorial to Carmen Mora, and, as I think she would have liked, that he say masses for her."

"So," Father William said sadly. "Carmen Mora is dead. We heard about her brother, of course, but . . ."

"Yes. She's dead," Doc said curtly. He didn't want to talk about it. It still hurt too much. He took his leave then. Father William wanted him to stay to discuss the wonderful things the money would do for the mission, but Doc didn't want to face the inevitable questions. He said his goodbyes, mounted, and continued east, the last of the gold jingling in his saddlebags.

He and Raider and their new escort had successfully delivered to Lord Crowley the remainder of the gold that Valdez had not already spent. But Doc had put in a claim for the reward. Nor for himself, of course. As an agent working on the case, he was not eligible, nor was Raider. He made the claim in the name of Carmen Mora. Now he was delivering it to her in the only way he could think of.

Later that day the Pala Mission came into sight. Doc could see old Padre Gregorio pottering about in his cactus garden. It was a lovely scene, the kind of scene he'd come to connect with southern California.

It took a very short time to complete his business with the old Mexican priest, but finally, a last goodbye to the old padre and he was ready to go. But go where?

Doc sat his horse, staring east. He wondered if he had the courage to continue on to Rancho La Libertad, on toward Diego and the vaqueros. He doubted it. It would be too painful; there were too many memories. No, they didn't need him there anyway. They had the rancho, the land, the animals, their culture. As for himself, with Carmen gone, he had nothing.

Nothing but his work, that is. Turning his horse west, he started back toward the coast. Toward the outside world.

J.D. HARDIN

"THE MOST EXCITING
WESTERN WRITER SINCE
LOUIS L'AMOUR"
—JAKE LOGAN

____ 872-16869-7	THE SPIRIT AND THE FLESH	$1.95
____ 867-21226-8	BOBBIES, BAUBLES AND BLOOD	$2.25
____ 06572-3	DEATH LODE	$2.25
____ 06380-1	THE FIREBRANDS	$2.25
____ 06410-7	DOWNRIVER TO HELL	$2.25
____ 06001-2	BIBLES, BULLETS AND BRIDES	$2.25
____ 06331-3	BLOODY TIME IN BLACKTOWER	$2.25
____ 06248-1	HANGMAN'S NOOSE	$2.25
____ 06337-2	THE MAN WITH NO FACE	$2.25
____ 06151-5	SASKATCHEWAN RISING	$2.25
____ 06412-3	BOUNTY HUNTER	$2.50
____ 06743-2	QUEENS OVER DEUCES	$2.50
____ 07017-4	LEAD-LINED COFFINS	$2.50
____ 08013-7	THE WYOMING SPECIAL	$2.50
____ 07259-2	THE PECOS DOLLARS	$2.50
____ 07257-6	SAN JUAN SHOOTOUT	$2.50
____ 07379-3	OUTLAW TRAIL	$2.50
____ 07392-0	THE OZARK OUTLAWS	$2.50
____ 07461-7	TOMBSTONE IN DEADWOOD	$2.50
____ 07381-5	HOMESTEADER'S REVENGE	$2.50
____ 07386-6	COLORADO SILVER QUEEN	$2.50
____ 07790-X	THE BUFFALO SOLDIER	$2.50
____ 07785-3	THE GREAT JEWEL ROBBERY	$2.50
____ 07789-6	THE COCHISE COUNTY WAR	$2.50
____ 07974-0	THE COLORADO STING	$2.50
____ 08032-3	HELL'S BELLE	$2.50

Prices may be slightly higher in Canada.

BERKLEY   *Available at your local bookstore or return this form to:*
Book Mailing Service
P.O. Box 690, Rockville Centre, NY 11571

Please send me the titles checked above. I enclose _____. Include 75¢ for postage and handling if one book is ordered; 25¢ per book for two or more not to exceed $1.75. California, Illinois, New York and Tennessee residents please add sales tax.

NAME _____

ADDRESS _____

CITY _____ STATE/ZIP _____

(allow six weeks for delivery.)